Three Days with Mary

And Other Stories

by
Michael Canavan

Fiction by Michael Canavan

The Nature Of the Beast

Non-fiction by Michael Canavan

What Does It Mean To Me?
*24 Hidden Rules Worksheets to Help Children
with Asperger's Syndrome Learn Social Skills*

Recognizing and Preventing Alcohol Abuse

Coping with Divorce: Activities for Men

Coping with Divorce: Activities for Children

Coping with Divorce: Activities for Women

Social Skills Comics: Conversational Skills in School

Social Skills Comics: Handling Anxiety in School

ISBN: 1493691759
ISBN-13: 978-1493691753

For Dylan, Taylor, and Reese.

CONTENTS

Three Days with Mary

MICHAEL CANAVAN

Friday Morning

The same thought came to him every time. He only had to look around the small room he had occupied for six years and just like that it popped into his head – it's a good thing no one ever comes up here. Even though there was no one to see what he saw, let alone judge it, he could still feel uncomfortable at times.

The stack of boxes was the culprit. They made him feel more than a little self-conscious. It was as if simply having them in there branded him conceited, or full of himself. Even relegated to the far corner as they were, he felt they still managed to scream, "Look at me!" After all it was a small room, and they were big boxes.

But really, what choice did he have? As the author of three books – three well-read and fairly controversial books - he had to keep at least a few on hand for days when he was asked for a signed copy, or for days when he was preparing to attend a conference where he would be challenged to defend some of the views expressed in his books, like that day. Those challenges came often, and not only at conferences. Any time, any where he was recognized would do. "They're not my views," he was often tempted to say at such times, "They're the Church's views. I just happen to agree with them. I just happen to be good at explaining them."

Of course Fr. Jack Fitzgerald, Fitz or Fr. Fitz to almost everyone who knew him, never said anything even remotely like that. He was far too even-tempered a man to give such a sarcastic sounding answer, and he loved debating far too much to ever cop out like that or let an opportunity to wrangle get away from him quite so easily.

He was looking forward to the next few days - there would be plenty of opportunities to wrangle where he was going. "Priest or Priestess" was the title of a two day conference being held in New York, the latest in a series staged in cities around the country to consider an expanded role for women in the Catholic Church, up to and including ordaining women as priests. Among the 'pro' speakers would be several nuns who felt they were called to do more for the Church than they were currently allowed, historians who never seemed to run out of examples of women who already had done more, usually without the Church's consent or knowledge, and a lawyer who was well-known for his courtroom victories in sex discrimination cases.

Fr. Fitzgerald was one of several speakers making up the 'con' camp, on hand to define and defend the Church's position, and to bathe that position in the best possible historical light – his specialty. The books he wrote on the subject of women in the Church throughout its history attracted a large number of readers, and they also polarized them – anyone who read his books either loved or hated every word.

But his readers' feelings about him were simpler. He was a recognized and respected authority on the subject, and he enjoyed a reputation as a sincere man among both camps. Because of that, and because he never deviated from Church teaching, he was called upon fairly regularly to be the face and voice of the Church whenever and wherever the issue was being debated.

But that was only part of what he did. He also had what he called his regular day job, working as a sort of chaplain-at-large in hospitals throughout the Archdiocese of New York. It always pained him to take time away from this work in order to attend conferences – there was no easy way to tell patients or their families that he would be going away the day before an operation, or when sacraments were being requested. But he did it because he believed he was writing and speaking about a vital issue. He considered it important work.

He also got a kick out of it. However it might have sounded, he would readily admit when asked that engaging what he referred to as the Other Side – the promoters of a female priesthood – was a gas.

But there was no engaging on the agenda that day, the Friday before the conference. On that day his plan was simply to drop off some of his books in the auditorium and check to make sure everything was ready. The real fun would begin on Monday when the conference actually got under way.

He had been receiving friendly warnings about what he was in for at this particular conference for the last few weeks – phone calls from friends and colleagues telling him to be prepared. He was going to find himself front-and-center, thrust into the spotlight like never before they were saying.

He listened to them politely and thanked them for their concern, but in truth they weren't telling him anything he didn't already know. His latest book, *The First Mary*, had been taking heavy fire from the Other Side since it came out two months before. That was all the warning he needed.

Besides, he wasn't being thrust at all if truth be told. He

had stepped into the spotlight all by himself. He knew he was doing it even as he was writing the book, but he saw no way to avoid it – it was a topic that needed clarifying in his view. In *The First Mary*, Fr. Fitz recounted how in 1979 Sister Theresa Kane, president of the Leadership Conference of Women Religious publicly requested that Pope John Paul II consider 'the possibility of women being included in all ministries of the church.' He then went on to make a case for backing up the Pope's indirect response in which he referred to Mary, the mother of Jesus saying, 'The model Mary represents clearly shows what is specific to the feminine personality. Indeed Mary is the model of full development of woman's vocation.'

In other words, equal but different. Women who wished to serve the Church should not try to do it by taking on a man's role, but by following the example set by the rather passive and subservient mother of Jesus. Why? Because they're made that way.

Championing that argument would have been enough to hit the Other Side where they live, but he went further. The second half of the book was devoted to discouraging women from idolizing other, more independent female characters in the Bible such as that other well-known Mary, Mary Magdalene. He did this by comparing the way they had been portrayed in contemporary books and movies with the more sedate Church traditions – the 'official' versions.

He thought of this as little more than a history lesson, but not surprisingly it was seen by many as a put-down of the beloved figures they modeled themselves on. Fr. Fitz knew there would be a few at the conference who would try to hit him with that charge, and he knew he was going to have to spend an inordinate amount of time mollifying them. He didn't mind - such was the price of success.

But one thing he had little patience for was the press, most of whom he found to be blatantly one-sided. In one particularly harsh review of the book he was actually accused of deliberately painting a less-than-flattering portrait of Mary Magdalene, and of going so far as to question her importance as an historical figure. Those charges bothered him greatly. He may not have thought of her - or the "her" portrayed in the numerous stories that have grown up about her - as role model material, but he certainly thought of her as an important figure. What's more, he recognized her as a beloved companion of Jesus' inner circle and a deeply intelligent and spiritual person. He was certain his writing made that clear and he felt that anyone misinterpreting his views on her was doing so intentionally.

He identified a number of writers as belonging to that camp, and he reflected a great deal on their use of tv shows, newspapers, blogs, and Lord-only-knew-what other kind of outlet to distort his opinions in order to assert their own. As a priest he prayed dutifully that they might learn to use their power in a more honest way. As a man he often thought that a good smack in the mouth might just do the trick.

He also reflected often on the many times he had been personally attacked in the press for his views since he published his first book several years ago. At various times and for various reasons he had been called sexist, misogynist, a dinosaur and worse. But he was a practical man, and he found it easy to ignore such attacks because he simply didn't buy any of it. His conscience was clear.

Besides, he reminded himself, people who said such things to him or about him were hopelessly generalizing. They were distorting not only his views on the issue, but the issue itself. To his mind it was not about sexism, feminism, or even equal rights. It was about women wanting to serve the

Church as priests, and nothing more. He was against that for specific reasons, but he held no similar views regarding women in the secular world – he had no issue with the idea of a woman being elected president, women serving in the military, even as commanders, or women in charge of boardrooms. He even had friends among the women who often opposed him at these conferences, and he respected them and the work they did. He simply thought they were wrong on the issue they debated.

As a seminarian he had been taught a simple thing which he still believed - the rationale for a male priesthood stemmed from the example set by Jesus himself, who charged a group of men, and only men with preaching His message. On more than one occasion it had been pointed out to Fr. Fitz that this was hardly proof of His intentions. True, he would answer, but since it seemed unlikely that anyone would be going back to ask Jesus exactly what He had in mind, it would have to do.

Besides, Pope John Paul II had laid the matter to rest in 1994 when he declared that the Church has no power to ordain women. Personally, Fr. Fitz saw no reason for there to be any continued discussion about it after that, particularly among the faithful since John Paul declared his judgment should be definitively held by them. But for whatever reason there was. There always was. The mere mention of women hoping to serve as Catholic priests someday always seemed to capture people's imaginations.

It wasn't hard to keep that kind of discussion going in books, the press, and at conferences like this one if the effort was well organized. And the Other Side was nothing, if not well organized. They did a very good job of promoting their cause. In the face of that effort, Fr. Fitz felt the Church needed someone who was willing to step up to the plate and speak for them. And in him the Church had just the guy, a man who was truly cut out for the job.

In addition to being very knowledgeable on the subject he also brought to the table the kinds of things that always seem simultaneously superficial and important. He was a very tall, good looking man, not yet forty, with a voice and a demeanor that every TV producer, conference organizer, and photographer loved. Plus, he was no talking head simply spouting the party line ad nauseum – he was the real thing. He meant every word, and it showed.

And he was generally regarded as fearless. He could be counted on to go toe-to-toe with the Other Side anytime, anywhere. Sometimes that meant a pleasant exchange with an articulate professional, and sometimes it meant being shouted down by zealots. It made no difference to him. As he got ready that morning he was preparing himself for both, and everything in between.

He grabbed a half-dozen copies of each of his books from the offending boxes and put them into a simple shopping bag, smiling as he did so. He was known to carry everything around in either shopping bags or an old thread-bare back pack he'd had for years. He had two handsome black briefcases he could have used instead, both sitting on a shelf high up in his closet. Both were brand new. Both had been given to him as gifts from colleagues – one of them even came with a note that read, "Hang up the back pack, high school was a long time ago." But he preferred to stick with what he knew. For dropping off books, he figured a shopping bag would do.

Picking it up, he left his room and headed down the stairs and out the front door, into the bright warmth of the late morning summer sun. He had a few stops to make before heading to the hotel where the conference was being held and he was glad to be getting an early start.

He stretched out one long arm to flag down a taxi – never an easy thing to do on a weekday in New York, even harder on the quiet little street where he lived at the rectory of Immaculate Conception Church in lower Manhattan. But that day he got lucky. Almost immediately he was climbing into the back of a cab, setting his bag on the seat beside him, and giving directions to the driver.

By then he was beginning to feel something he had been waiting for, something that always crept up on him in the days leading up to a public appearance and made him think of certain patients he had counseled as a chaplain. Naturally, many of the older patients were veterans of one war or another – World War II, Korea, sometimes even Viet Nam. He spent a great deal of time with them, praying with them, receiving the latest news from their doctors with them, good and bad, and when they needed to talk, listening to them. That, most of all.

Almost all those veterans had been out of the service for decades, but they still seemed to hold tight to their most graphic war-time memories. And when they got scared those memories became even more vivid, and then they wanted to talk about them. Most talked about things you would expect, like the terrifying battles they had fought in or the great friends they made who never saw their twenty-first birthday.

But sometimes they came out with completely unexpected things, like how they lived for going into battle. That wasn't something he heard too often – in fact, only a few said it over the years, but those few were enough to make a lasting impression.

The stories differed - some were more detailed than others, like the one about the guy who only wanted walk point whenever his unit was on patrol. But there was a common theme to them, and it wasn't anything as dark as a death wish. It was a sense of justification or righteousness. They were looking to make sense of the sacrifices they and their buddies were making, and they couldn't do it tucked safely away in the rear. But they could do it climbing out of a foxhole. They could do it where the bullets were flying.

That idea always stuck with him, and not because it was so fantastic. Just the opposite. While he would never have dared to liken himself to them or compare his experiences to theirs, he nevertheless felt that he could understand, if only in some small way the feeling they were trying to describe. The attitude. That was his word, not theirs, but it worked for him.

He could feel that attitude growing in him as he pulled the cab door closed behind him. He knew that gearing up for one of these appearances was as close as he would ever come to climbing out of a fox hole, but so be it. This was the fight he had chosen to fight. And if he was about to come under attack as he had been warned, all the better. This would be his chance to feel righteous.

He believed he was ready for anything. He would continue to believe that for a short while longer.

Friday Afternoon

Fr. Fitz arrived at the hotel a little after three o'clock. As he neared the front door he happened to catch a glimpse of himself in the hotel's floor-to-ceiling windows, and without even meaning to he stopped to consider his reflection. Towering there, his long black suit topped by a head of black hair and his shopping bag of books dangling at his side, he thought to himself, "Man, you look ridiculous." That feeling would only be compounded a moment later.

While he was still appraising himself he heard what sounded like someone tapping on glass. He turned to see two pretty faces looking back at him through the window of the hotel bar, each one wearing a smile that said, "I caught you checking yourself out." One of the smiles he didn't recognize, but the other he knew only too well. It belonged to Marianne Boyle, one of the most articulate professionals the Other Side had to offer. He assumed she must have come into town early in order to check out the auditorium just as he was doing.

What could he do but hang his head and laugh? It certainly wouldn't improve things if he tried to sputter out some lame explanation – "No, no, I wasn't looking at myself, really..." Marianne began to point and jab in the direction of the lobby, inviting him to come in and join them. With a smile and a short wave he agreed, using his own impromptu sign language to say he would go in and drop off his things first.

When she nodded her understanding he entered the hotel and got into the elevator, heading for the auditorium on the third floor.

As soon as the doors closed he slumped against the wall and let out a deep sigh. He hadn't expected to run into Marianne before Monday, and he didn't like being caught off guard like that. Knowing when and where their paths would cross was important to him - it was how he coped.

Marianne Boyle was a former history teacher who lived and worked in Boston. He had known her professionally for over five years. During that time they had sat on opposite sides of various podiums, and appeared across from each other on a number of news shows and talk radio programs.

Their professional relationship was built on a single principle – disagreement. Yet despite that, and despite the fact that they only saw each other two or three times a year they had managed to become close friends. Adversary or not, he respected her commitment and her skill. On a personal level he enjoyed being in her company, and found her very easy to talk to and even easier to listen to. He also loved her. In another situation 'in love' would have been the better expression, but in this one 'love' would have to do.

He found nothing wrong with that, felt no guilt whatsoever. After all, he didn't choose to love any more than the next man. For that matter he didn't choose it any more than any other priest who experienced the same thing. It happened sometimes, and it had happened to him.

The Church is well aware that its priests are sometimes forced to deal with feelings of love or physical attraction. Their teaching on the subject is actually very understanding, and just as straightforward. Rather than beat himself up over it, a priest who finds himself in that situation is simply encouraged to manage it by channeling his emotions into an appropriate friendship. His feelings shouldn't be revealed to the person he is attracted to, and certainly should never be acted upon. If he is forced to be in frequent contact with the other person and keeping his feelings to himself proves too difficult, then he is expected to remove himself from the situation altogether. To move.

Fr. Fitz considered himself extremely fortunate in that regard. Marianne was not a parishioner, didn't even live in the same state. He had been successfully managing the situation for years without ever letting on in any way, without ever saying a word to her about his feelings.

What would be the point? He was a priest. He dealt with the thoughts whenever they came up - thoughts about a very different kind of life he could have lived with her, a life in which he hadn't accepted his vocation. But he had accepted it, and at the end of the day they were no more than that, thoughts. He was a priest. Period.

Plus, he was very practical. The way he saw it, being reminded that he could have made other choices, followed other paths, only strengthened his commitment to this one. He felt privileged to know her and work with her, privileged in a sense to be challenged by being in her presence at these functions, and just as privileged to walk away from each and every encounter feeling right, happy in the sacrifices he made, and convinced that he was living his life the way it was meant to be lived.

She had been on his mind more than usual that week because he was expecting to see a good deal of her during the conference. As was usual whenever she was going to be around, he was going down two tracks simultaneously - even as he was preparing to refute nearly every point she might make before an audience, he was spending more time straightening his clerical collar and checking his hair in the mirror before he left the rectory each morning.

He had to smile whenever he caught himself doing that. Dealing with such conflicting thoughts was stressful, but it could also be good for a laugh provided you're any good at laughing at yourself, which he was. It's a burden, he always thought at such times, but it does keep me on my toes.

By the time the elevator doors opened, he had more or less recovered from the shock of seeing her. He had been in this situation before he reminded himself, and it could have been much worse. For one thing she wasn't alone. Even one other person was a welcome distraction. For another, she was in a public place. He didn't like bars generally, which was not surprising since he didn't drink. But they were loud, busy places – more distractions.

A bar also made it easy for him to keep it short. He would tell her he could only stay for one drink. After that he would say goodbye and walk away as he always did - without guilt, without fear, and grateful for the experience.

Fifteen minutes later things were working out as planned. More or less. The three of them were sitting around a table towards the rear of the bar, enjoying a nice private conversation. More or less. The sight of two attractive women and a priest sharing a drink together in a bar, and having a good time at that was enough to attract the curious attention of a number of the bar's patrons. Some were subtle – they pretended to be looking casually around the bar in order to steal quick glances when they could. Others were not so subtle - they just looked.

Even sitting with his back turned to much of the room, Fr. Fitz was not unaware of the attention – he tended to draw a lot of stares even when he wasn't sitting with pretty women, and he had a good sense for it after all these years. Personally, he couldn't have cared less. It had never bothered him. He was just glad that his companions either didn't notice or didn't mind.

Besides, he could easily imagine what made the people in the bar look, the types of things they were wondering. What do the young women see in this priest? What does the priest see (that he shouldn't be seeing) in these young women? Was a priest even allowed to be in a bar? Was there was such a thing as 'off-duty' for a priest?

In a way, he found the attention amusing. What was ironic, he thought, was that whatever was going on in their imaginations was far racier than anything going on at his table – even the glass in front of him held only orange juice, which was the hardest thing he ever drank.

He had finished about half of it since sitting down, and in that time he had also good-naturedly taken all the teasing that came his way about having been 'busted' staring at his reflection in the hotel window. He had also been introduced to Marianne's friend Becca Nolan, a recent New York University grad and freelance writer who was there to cover the conference. He was pleased to find her knowledgeable about the topic of the upcoming debate, but more or less detached professionally. As part of her preparation she had even read his latest book, which she said she found fascinating.

"Thank you very much, that's kind of you to say. Just curious - you weren't offended by anything I wrote?"

She looked surprised by the question. "Why? I never wanted to be a priest."

No answer could have pleased him more. He took being misunderstood in stride, but it was still nice to come across someone every now and again who could read his books without reading into them. "Thank you," he said again.

Fr. Fitz was enjoying the conversation so much that he

ended up staying a bit longer than he had planned. He was so busy answering all Becca's questions about the conference – how it was organized, how civil the participants were likely to be, what he saw as his role in it - that it took him even longer than it took Becca to notice that Marianne had stopped talking. What they both actually became aware of was not her silence, but what she was doing - she was fidgeting with her blouse, pulling at the shoulders and unfastening, then refastening the top button.

She seemed unaware that she was being watched until Becca stopped in mid-sentence and leaned toward her, smiling. "What's the matter?" she asked. "Ants in your pants... your shirt?"

"What? No, no... I just shouldn't have worn this blouse. I didn't realize it showed so much cleavage." Then, realizing what she had just said Marianne turned to Fr. Fitz and put a hand over her mouth and gave a little nervous laugh. She started to apologize, but he simply waved her off.

Far from being offended, he could have thanked her. Sometimes it took just such an accidental remark, but it was exactly at moments like that, when people were not tip-toeing around him that he felt most able to be himself. And as himself, he simply responded to what she said with the first thing that came to mind. "It doesn't show too much. You look very professional. Very beautiful, as always."

She took her time answering. "Thank you, Fitz," she said with a warm smile.

"Of course. Besides, it's a pretty blouse. I think that cut suits you."

When he saw that Becca was staring at him across the table he asked, "Not the answer you expected?"

"From a priest? Not really, no."

"Why? It's only natural to appreciate beauty."

"Yes, I know. I didn't mean that, I meant the other thing... That cut suits you? I'm sure I've never heard a priest give fashion advice before."

"Oh. Well, priests are no strangers to fashion. Why do you think we always wear black?"

"Because it goes with everything? Ha, ha. Very funny."

Fr. Fitz laughed out loud, pleased with his own humor. That brought a few more glances from around the room. Marianne took a sip from her drink and said, "Like I told you Becca, Fr. Fitz here is not your typical priest, not by a long shot. And it's not just his highly developed sense of fashion that sets him apart, either."

"Is it the fact that he's an Irish-American priest who doesn't drink?"

"Ha! I wasn't even thinking about that, but no, that's not what I meant."

"I don't know, I think I'm fairly typical," Fr. Fitz said.

Marianne turned to him. "Oh, no you're not, Fitz. There's not another priest that I've ever been able to talk to the way I can talk to you."

If you could only imagine, he thought, what it means to me to hear you say that.

"You just said it, a priest is a man first. I wish I always felt that, but I don't. You're the only one."

That was almost too much. Part of him considered getting up to leave right then and there, but he managed to hold it together and answer her. "That's very nice of you to say, Marianne. Thank you."

"You're welcome. You know, I'll bet it has something to do with you receiving your calling late, like you once told me."

"Late?" asked Becca.

Marianne gestured for him to take over his own story.

"Fitz?"

He smiled. "Well, not late really, but later than most, I guess. Most priests I know had some idea of what they were being called to do even before they were teenagers – not a complete picture maybe but a hint, some feeling. They had years to deal with it. Years to seek advice, to grow into the idea, even to explore different paths. But I was twenty before it ever hit me, and when it did it happened all at once. Almost overnight."

"Twenty. Really? You didn't even think about it before then?"

"No, never once. I was always very involved with the Church, and I often thought I would end up working for it in some way. At times I even considered becoming a deacon, but I never saw myself becoming a priest. I saw my future very clearly, and it wasn't that. I thought that I would have a family, that I would marry, raise children, live in a community, not separate as I do now."

"You saw all that?"

"I saw it, yes, and I wanted it very much, right up until I was twenty." He nodded towards Marianne. "That's what she's referring to."

Becca was waiting for more, but he had stopped speaking. "Well, what changed your mind?" she asked.

"You mean how did I end up becoming a priest?"

"Yes, what happened when you were twenty? If you don't mind me asking…"

"No, not at all."

"Wow, this is exciting," Marianne said, "I don't think you've ever told me this part, Fitz".

"No? Well, it was nothing too far-fetched, really. My father died when I was twenty. That's what started it. Well no, that isn't really true. It actually started when he got sick, when he was in the hospital."

"What did he have?"

"Well, it was just headaches at first. At least that's what he told me. I found out later he'd been having terrible headaches every day for months and hadn't said anything. He was a tough old guy - you know the type – he didn't hold with 'running off to doctors for every little thing,' as he would say, so…

But then things started happening that he couldn't hide. His speech became slurred, he began to feel tired all the time and he started losing a lot of weight. When it got to where his clothes looked like they were just hanging on him he finally gave in and let me take him to get checked out.

"The news was bad, of course. He had lung cancer which had spread to his brain. That's what was causing the headaches and all the rest. It had even spread to his bones."

He waved his hand over his chest.

"Of course, it was too late to do anything about it. He might have had a chance if it had been discovered earlier, but by then all we could do was wait. That was the hardest part of the whole thing for me. Knowing he was going to die, but not knowing exactly when – a month, two…

"I left school to care for him as much as I could, but there really wasn't much of anything I could do. His doctors, too. Aside from making him comfortable there really wasn't anything for them to do, either.

"Most of the time there was only me there with my father… me and the hospital's chaplain who would come by every day, sometimes more than once to spend some time with us and pray with us. He was such a great guy - Fr. Ponce De Leon was his name. All of about five-foot-four, maybe sixty years old, with a thick head of white hair. Just a pleasant, reassuring sort of character, exactly what I always thought a priest should be – not like me at all."

He shot a quick smile at his companions.

"You know, I found out later that he drove an hour each way to get to the hospital. And he did that every day. Absolutely amazing. I didn't even know he was coming the first day he showed up. It was just a quick thirty minute surprise visit, but I felt so much better afterwards that I couldn't wait for him to come back. In no time I came to rely on them. Towards the end I think I would have been a wreck without them, to be honest.

"Well, as it turned out my father passed away in less than a month. It was for the better, all things considered. Fr. Ponce – that was what people called him – was there with me right at the end. After it was all over, I was just so grateful to him for all that he had been able to do for us both, spiritually and emotionally. I was so moved by it that I found myself wanting to do the very same thing for others who were ill, and for their families, their sons. At first I wasn't even sure how to go about such a thing. I spoke to him about it, but only once. He didn't push me one way or another, just made suggestions for things I could read, people I could talk to, ways I might explore my conscience.

"A lot of possible futures entered my mind as a result, and then left again just as quickly. I even toyed with the idea of joining the army to become a chaplain. That seemed like a good way to help a lot of people, but I couldn't get my mind around the idea, somehow. It seemed like a half-measure. I kept feeling that I wasn't supposed to do something like what Fr. Ponce did, I was supposed to do exactly what he did, as if the perfect example had been shown to me. So in the end..."

"Instead of young Fitz becoming Captain Fitzgerald, he became Fr. Fitzgerald," Marianne interjected.

"Something like that, yes."

"Good," she teased him, "because the army would have caught off all that gorgeous hair."

He smiled at that, then shrugged. "And that was it. It all happened just that quickly. Before my father's passing I had never thought of joining the priesthood, but within an hour of it I was. A week later I was decided."

Becca was quiet for a moment but she clearly had something more on her mind. "So, then everything changed for you... you had to go to the seminary?"

"Yup. I went to St. Joseph's right up the road here, in Yonkers."

"And you had to... you had to give up everything else in order to do that?"

"What do you mean?"

Becca hesitated. "I'm sorry, I was going to ask you a fairly personal question."

"That's okay."

"But you – priests, I mean – you must have people asking you personal questions all the time just to see if you're really human."

He smiled. "Or to see if we're actually a race of angels or something."

"Exactly my point. But that's not why I was going to ask what I was going to ask..."

He held out his hands. "By all means, ask away."

"Well, you were twenty when you got your calling. You were looking forward to a life where you would have a wife and children. I hope this isn't inappropriate, but did you have a girlfriend?"

Fr. Fitz smiled and sat back. After a moment he answered. "No, it's not inappropriate at all. And the answer is yes, I did. And to answer your first question, yes, I had to give her up."

"Fitz," Marianne said in a soft voice. "I never knew that."

"No? Well, I guess you don't possess Becca's keen journalistic instinct for a hot story."

"No, I guess not. Well, what happened between you and, and your friend…?"

"Natalie."

"Natalie. Unless that's too personal…"

"Personal, no. Embarrassing is more like it. The fact is wherever Natalie is, whatever she's doing, I'm sure she'd like to know the very same thing – what happened. This was almost twenty years ago, mind you. I'd like to think I've grown a bit since then. I would never do to anyone else what I did to her."

"Sounds bad, Fitz."

"Well, once I decided I was going to enter the seminary I had to break up with her, as Becca points out. And, well… I did. With absolutely no warning, mind you. I simply called her up one evening – I can still remember how happy her voice sounded when she answered the phone – and without mincing words I said goodbye. I don't think I was on the phone for more than two minutes. After that I simply disappeared from her life. We never spoke again after that day – not by phone, by letter, by e-mail… nothing."

"Really. She didn't try to get in touch with you again?"

"Oh, she did, yeah. For a couple of weeks she called the house almost every day. And she wrote me a letter. It was handwritten, all nine pages of it."

"Nine pages!" Marianne exclaimed.

"Uh, huh. Back and front."

"Wow. Well, she clearly wasn't ready to let go. What did she write?"

"I don't recall. This and that. All she really wanted was to know why, to understand what had happened. That was fair. I knew owed her an explanation, but I never answered the phone, not even once. And I never responded to her letter, either."

"She didn't agree with you joining the priesthood?" Becca asked.

"I wouldn't know. I never told her I was going to."

Marianne exchanged a surprised glance with Becca before asking, "What do you mean?"

Fr. Fitz laughed. "Just that. When I called her that last time I said I was going away and we had to break up. I didn't tell her why. I didn't tell her what I was doing."

"I don't understand. Why not?"

"I don't really know. Maybe I was afraid she would try to talk me out of it. I didn't want her to do that. Maybe that wasn't the reason – I really don't know."

Becca was ready with the next question. "Were you two serious? How long had you been together?"

"A little over two years."

"Two years! And you just left? Ouch."

"Not my proudest moment, believe me. Here I was going off to become a priest so I could minister to the sick and dying, yet I acted with very little compassion towards someone I truly cared about. I didn't understand it while I was doing it. Still don't."

They were quiet for a while after that. Then it was Marianne's turn to laugh. "Oh, Fitz. I knew you were full of surprises even after all this time, but a heartbreaker? My, my. What did I tell you, Becca? Not your typical priest."

Becca was laughing, too. "No." After taking a sip of her drink, she offered another thought. "But she probably knows by now, don't you think, Fr. Fitz?"

"Sorry?"

"Natalie. She must know by now that you're a priest. I mean, you've been on television quite a bit in the last few years, you're always being interviewed and written about, and so on. If she hasn't spotted your picture in a book store, or come across an article about you in a magazine in some doctor's waiting room, I'd be very surprised. I'm sure she put two and two together long ago."

The thought had certainly occurred to him. He had prayed for that very thing countless times. "I hope so. I really do."

"I'm sure of it," she continued. "And I'll bet she's happy to know it. After all, what woman wouldn't rather lose her man to God than say, just another woman? It's a lot easier on the ego." More laughs all around. More stares from the observers.

Fr. Fitz would never have guessed he would be talking about any of that when he sat down. As far as he could recall he had never told the story about Natalie to anyone, at least not without some serious editing. It had never seemed worth sharing before. But given the circumstances, he could understand why he had been so willing that day. Telling it had enabled him to escape the awkwardness of the present situation by slipping into the past, even if it was an embarrassing past. All things being equal, it was a good trade.

They went on to other topics after that, but both Marianne and Becca had their own preparations to get to in advance of the conference and so they said their goodbyes a short while later. While she was gathering her things Becca told Fr. Fitz and Marianne that she was looking forward to seeing the flip side of their relationship. Having witnessed the charming and unexpected spectacle of the priest and the feminist sharing stories over a drink like old dear friends, she could only wonder what it was going to be like to see them in action opposing each other, painting each other as misguided or misinformed. Mostly though, she looked forward to observing how they reconciled the two sides of their relationship. Fr. Fitz couldn't help but smile at that, and simply said he hoped she had ring-side seats.

After they had gone he sat back down just long enough to finish his orange juice and give a quiet word of thanks that he was walking away from yet another encounter with Marianne more or less unscathed, feeling grateful for the experience and nothing else. When he was done he got up and walked to the bar to ask for his bill.

While he was waiting to pay he leaned back with his elbows on the bar and scanned the room, taking a look at some of the people who had been taking a look at him for the last half hour. Not surprisingly, every one of them was now looking up, down, anywhere but in his direction, doing their best to avoid meeting his eyes. No one seemed to be aware of the basketball player-sized priest any more now that he was standing just a few feet away, looking in their direction. Except for one.

Out of the corner of his eye he caught a quick glance from the other side of the bar. It came from one of the farthest tables where four men dressed in business suits sat together talking over beers. Feeling mischievous, he gave a nod in their direction. "How's it goin'?" he bellowed across the room. Suddenly all eyes were on them as they looked around the room nervously, then back at him, startled and uncertain. He nodded again and gave them a thumbs up. "Cheers!" he said, in the same loud voice. That forced a few half-hearted nods from the poor guys who expected anything but to suddenly be the center of attention, and were probably wondering where the hidden cameras were.

Happy with his little bit of mischief-making he turned

back to the bar, smiling to himself. He thanked the bartender and collected his change, then headed out the same way he came in, through the hotel lobby.

But by the time he got half-way across the room his smile had all but faded. His mischievous attitude was also gone, replaced within the space of those few steps by an unfamiliar feeling. He couldn't put his finger on it, but he could still feel himself reacting to it. He was slowing down. He no longer wanted to leave the hotel, but he had no idea why. Except for the feeling – the feeling that he had to stay, that there was something important waiting for him.

He didn't understand what it meant at first any more than he understood where it had come from, but it grew stronger and more clear with each step he took. By the time he left the bar and got as far as the front desk the vague feeling that something was waiting for him had grown into a fully formed idea - it wasn't something that was waiting for him, but someone. There was someone he was supposed to meet, someone who was waiting for him right there in the lobby.

Of course, the stronger it grew the harder he found it to accept. What was he talking about any way, a premonition? It made no sense that he should give such a thing any credence - he certainly didn't believe in any kind of fortune telling. But then it also made no sense that he should be standing in the middle of the lobby looking around with no idea who he was even looking for. And yet, whether he believed in it or not that was exactly what he was doing.

He tried to look into as many faces as he could, but was no easy task. People were rushing by him in every direction, alone and in groups. For all he knew any one of them could have been the person he felt he was supposed to meet. Everyone stood out in one way or another at first, so after a while no one did. It was just a crowd he was watching. But when he looked down towards the far end of the lobby something finally caught his eye. Maybe.

He wasn't sure what he saw. At first he couldn't even be sure he had really seen anything at all. It was hard to make out anything through the people, there were so many of them. But when the crowd cleared a bit he saw that there was a small sitting area in the far corner. And sitting all by herself on one of the sofas – right where he somehow knew she would be - was someone. Someone looking directly at him, smiling at him.

"Excuse me?" said the clerk behind the desk.

Fr. Fitz turned. "I'm sorry, what?"

"You said 'Mary.'"

"Did I?"

"Yes," said the clerk, who clearly was not a Mary.

"Oh, I must have been daydreaming. I wasn't talking to you, sorry."

He turned back to her. She hadn't moved, hadn't even stopped smiling. Mary? Was that her name? How on earth could he know that? He met a lot of people in his work – patients and their families, participants at the many conferences where he spoke, reporters, readers at book signings – she could have been any of those, but she wasn't. He had never laid eyes on her before, he was sure of it. And yet, he had just said the word out loud, hadn't he? Mary. He did know it - her name was Mary. He knew it just like he knew that she was waiting for him. It made no sense that he would know any of it, but he did.

It also made no sense that he should walk up to her with no idea why he was doing it, but the feeling that he had to meet her was so strong that he didn't even bother to think twice. In fact, his only real concern as he made his way towards her was what he should say first when he got there. Should he address her as Mary, or keep that bit to himself for the time being? Should he demand to know what was going on, or play it cool and wait to see what happened? He never really decided, but it didn't matter. She said, "Hi," as soon as he got close, before he had a chance to say anything at all.

At first he only stared at her without answering. He hadn't noticed it when he first saw her from a distance, but up close she seemed almost out of place. She was young, maybe thirty, but she was dressed the way he imagined his mother might have dressed in high school in the early seventies – tall boots, a long skirt, a peasant blouse... like a hippie, he thought. She even had two braids in her long hair that wrapped around to the back like a headband.

"I'm sorry?" he finally stammered. It was the best he could manage.

She laughed and gave a little wave. "I said, hi."

"Right. Of course. Hi."

"Would you like to sit down?"

"Sure. Sure, thank you." He pulled up an arm chair, and sat down facing her.

He continued to look at her, hoping to see something that might help explain what had brought him to her, what he had been feeling for the last few minutes. But when she suddenly asked, "Am I not what you expected?" he was more confused, not less.

"I... I didn't expect anything," he said. Again, it was all he could come up with.

"Well, you're exactly what I expected, except I didn't know you would be so tall," she replied, as if she hadn't even heard him. "Of course, I had a head start. I've been aware of you for some time."

All he learned from that exchange was that she spoke with a southern accent.

"I'm sorry, I don't understand. You've been aware of me? Do you know me?"

She seemed puzzled by his questions. "Certainly, I know you. I'm here for you, to see you."

"You're here to see me? Why?"

"You mean you don't know?"

"No. No, I don't."

"But you're here. You came over to me."

"I did, yes, but quite frankly I don't why." He pointed over his shoulder to the bar. "I was in there, and I got this feeling that…"

"What?"

"That I had to meet somebody. You."

"That's all? Nothing else is coming to you?"

He only looked at her.

"Well, it will. It took a little while to come to me, but it did finally."

That seemed such a strange thing to say, he wondered if maybe she had the wrong person. It was hardly a reasonable explanation for what was happening, but it was better than none. "Are you sure you're looking for me? I'm Fr. Jack Fitzgerald," he said. For some reason he put out his hand as he said it.

She took his hand and laughed. Leaning in towards him she said, "I know who you are, Fitz. I told you, I came here to see you." After a moment she said, "And me? You're wondering who I am?"

"Yes, I am. But…"

"But you know who I am," she said. "You probably knew the moment you saw me."

He remembered what he said in front of the front desk clerk. "Mary. You're Mary," he said.

"Yes."

She was right, it was coming to him, only it felt more like he was coming to it. He didn't feel like he was learning anything new, more like he was recognizing what he had known all along.

Yet, the more the truth presented itself the more he tried to reject it and hold out for another, a truth that was easier to swallow. This doesn't make any sense, he kept thinking, it isn't possible. But even as he struggled with what could or couldn't be, he heard himself saying it again, declaring it. "You're Mary."

"Yes. I'm Mary. Mary Tour."

"Tour?"

She nodded. "Of course, I was called by another name at another time. But, you already know that, too."

Yes, he thought, I do know it. "Mary Magdalene."

"Yes, Fitz."

He shook his head. "But... how can that be? I don't understand."

"I don't understand either, but I know, and that's more important. I know it in my heart. How about you? What does your heart say?"

To hell with my heart, he wanted to say. I don't want to believe any of this, I don't know it. But he couldn't say that. It wasn't true. His heart said he did know it. He KNEW it. This woman sitting before him was Mary Magdalene. Whatever that meant, however that could be, she was here and she had come to see him.

When he didn't answer she guessed at the reason for his hesitation. "You're waiting for the sky to turn dark, aren't you? You're waiting for the earth to shake?" she asked him with a smile.

He could only nod at first. That was exactly what he was thinking - there had to be more to it.

"Maybe not that, but something, yes," he said finally. He gestured towards the crowds. "All these people are coming and going like nothing at all is happening, like it's just another day. And why wouldn't they? There's nothing here to see but you and me, just two people sitting down talking. I don't understand how there isn't something... I don't know, more. How can this be all there is to it?"

She answered him very gently. "Maybe this is all that's needed, if the right two people are doing the talking."

He could only shrug. "I guess." It wasn't the answer he was looking for - in fact it only raised more questions - but it was the kind of reasonable response he was prone to accept.

"What does your heart say, Fitz?" she asked him again.

And then just like that, what hadn't been enough suddenly was. Just as she said it would, it had come to him. He couldn't even find his full voice when he spoke again. He took her hand in his and answered her in something of a whisper.

"My heart says you're Mary, Mary of Magdala. It says you are the trusted Disciple of Our Lord who stayed with him while he was put to death, who was first to greet him when he rose... you are Mary."

She squeezed his hand. "Yes. Yes, I am. And I came here to see you."

Friday Evening

He might have been worried that their conversation would be overheard in the lobby. He might have felt that whatever was happening was simply too big for any place with walls. Whatever the reason, Fr. Fitz wanted to go. He suggested to Mary that they leave the hotel and take a walk outside.

He was immediately glad he did. As soon as he took his first breath of fresh air he began to feel more himself. His mind and his heart, both of which had been racing slowed to an easier pace to match the rhythm of their walking. Mary also seemed to be enjoying herself as they simply strolled around for a while in whatever direction the green lights took them. They could have been mistaken for just two more of the after-work crowd, but unlike them he and Mary were in no particular hurry to get anywhere, which is why he was surprised when they did.

When he realized they were standing on the corner of Fifth Avenue and fifty-eighth street he wondered if they really had arrived there entirely by chance, or if maybe he had been steering them that way all along without even realizing it. Either way, it seemed the ideal place to be and he happily guided Mary across the street and into Central Park.

Not once since they left the hotel had she pushed him to talk, or even to listen for that matter. She had a head start as she said, and whatever that meant he got the feeling that she was being patient with him, waiting for him to feel caught up.

But they hadn't been completely silent. He had learned one important thing from her as they walked – she didn't necessarily have the answers to all the questions running around in his head. Or her own. She knew why she was there, but only up to a point. She was there to see him. But why, or what was supposed to come of it she didn't know. She assumed the answers to those questions would become clear to one or both of them somehow, at some point. It both comforted and worried him to know that he wasn't the only one in the dark.

Still, he felt it was about time he said something, so he started with something he knew. "Beautiful, isn't it?" he asked her as they walked, making a sweeping gesture with his arm.

"The park? Yes, it is. Very beautiful."

"You know, Central Park divides the city in two. That's the west side over there. Those beautiful old buildings you see over the trees? That's Central Park West. There's a lake just over there, and where we just entered at the corner of Central Park South and…"

Mary laughed. "I know, Fitz. But it's nice of you to be such a gracious host."

"You know what, Central Park?"

"New York."

"How do you know New York?

"I live here."

He could feel his head tilt. "Here? In New York?"

"Yes. Why not?"

"I don't know. I guess I assumed you just got here, or appeared, or… I don't even know what I'm saying. So, you live in New York?"

"Yes. That is, I've been living here for a little while."

"Where?"

She pointed in the direction of the upper West Side.

"In, in a convent or something?"

She shook her head. "No, not in a convent or something. I'm not a nun, Fitz. I live in an apartment."

He stopped walking. "An apartment?"

She laughed again and tugged on his arm to continue.

"Yes, an apartment, all by myself like a big girl."

"Well, does anyone else…"

"Know who I am? No. No one knows but you."

"Well, how long have you been here?"

"I really can't say. I think a few weeks, at least."

"You think?"

"Some of my memories seem to go back that far, others… I don't know. It's very hard for me to say."

"Well, what about before that, before a few weeks ago? Do you remember anything from, you know… before?"

After a slight pause, she said, "Some things, yes. Not everything." She waited again before continuing. "It's the strangest thing. I don't know why, but what I do remember seems very recent. I understand that it's been many years, but it simply doesn't feel that way. It's the emotions. I feel things as if they happened just a short while ago. Certain things still feel wonderful, but others still hurt. Am I making any sense?"

"Yes, you are. And I'm sorry," he said.

She smiled, then said, "So, did you want to ask me about something in particular? You seem to be interested in an orderly timeline."

"I guess so. I was wondering how whatever went before turned into this for you. I mean, different stories have you living in different places in your later years - France, Turkey, even Rome… Whatever the real story is, how did that end and this begin? Or was there something, I don't know, in between? Is it alright that I ask that?"

"Yes, it's okay, but that I don't remember. I don't know where I was living in my 'later years' as you say. As far as what was in between..." She shook her head slowly. "I don't know. I feel certain things maybe, but they're things I can't talk about."

"Can't?"

"No, that's the wrong word. Maybe they're things that just aren't relevant, or shouldn't be relevant."

"Okay. Well then, what is relevant? Maybe knowing that has something to do with why you're here."

"Maybe." She thought for a minute, then added, "Yes, I'm sure you're right. We'll figure out what's relevant as we talk. We still have time."

"What do you mean?"

"We have two more days - tomorrow and Sunday."

"Two more days? Until what?"

"I have just three days to be with you."

"Three days? And after three days, what?"

"After that? Nothing. We have three days."

Fr. Fitz felt a sudden panic – in the dark is one thing, but out of time almost before they begin? He suddenly regretted the time they had spent leisurely walking around the city - it seemed like precious time wasted now. "Just a minute, let me understand this. We don't even know what you're doing here yet or what's supposed to happen, but we're on the clock already? How can that be?"

Mary shook her head. "We have three days," she said again.

"Okay, but what now? What do we do first? Were you given any sort of instructions? Do you know how we're supposed to begin?"

"We have begun, Fitz."

"What? Yes, I suppose so, but is there... I don't know... a map, a clue, something to tell us where to go, what to do next? Maybe there's some way we can petition for more time to figure this thing out. Can't we...?

He didn't finish his thought. They stood facing each other - she was the one who had stopped walking this time. She had both her hands over her mouth as she laughed at his outburst.

After a moment he had to laugh himself. "I'm sorry," he said.

She lowered her hands only long enough to echo his word. "Petition? Oh, Fitz."

He could only roll his eyes at how ridiculous that must have sounded. "I don't know. It just doesn't seem like enough."

She put her hand on his arm. "Fitz. It isn't a matter of enough. It isn't a matter of how much, or how little. All that matters is this - we have three days."

Friday Night

"Well?"

"Well…," then silence.

"Come on now, I need more than that. I need to know what you think."

Fr. Romero didn't move from his place on the sofa. In fact, he had barely moved a muscle in the hour since Fr. Fitz got home and sat him down in the living room to listen to his story.

In more than four decades as a parish priest Fr. Romero had learned a great deal about listening to people's stories. At that moment he was wondering what else he might have learned in all those years that would possibly help him deal with something like this.

Finally, he dropped his hand from his chin where it had been resting the whole time, the listening part of the conversation over. "Well. In all honesty, you've presented me with a real dilemma."

"How so?"

"On the one hand, after knowing you as long as I have I can honestly say that I would believe anything, absolutely anything you told me."

"Thank you."

"On the other hand you've just told me something which I simply can't believe. Perhaps I wouldn't want to believe it even if I could."

Fr. Fitz could only nod his understanding.

"I suppose there's no point in asking if she was able to offer you any sort of proof of her identity."

"Like what, a two thousand year old driver's license? Maybe an old utility bill with her name and address on it?"

Fr. Romero smiled and shook his head. "I see your point."

"Besides, who she is isn't a question, Father. I know who she is. I knew it even before she said a single word. I said her name as soon as I laid eyes on her." When Fr. Romero didn't answer right away, he continued. "Believe me, I know how this sounds… 'Hey, how was your day?' 'Great! I had a long chat with Mary Magdalene. Yeah, she picked me up in mid-town and we took a nice stroll through the park.' I know. But it's a fact."

Fr. Romero only nodded, then got down to business. "Well, let's just say it is. In that case I suppose my first question would be the same as yours. Why is she here? What does she want? What does she hope to accomplish in three days?"

"Precisely."

"My second would be, why you? She said she came here just to see you. But why? In all likelihood you weren't chosen at random, but because something about you makes you suitable for whatever her purpose here is.

"So the question really is, what does she hope to accomplish in three days with you?"

Fr. Fitz had no answer for that. Not yet.

"Tell me," Fr. Romero continued, "where is this apartment of hers? Exactly."

"I don't know."

"You didn't ask, or she wouldn't say?"

He thought for a moment. "I don't really remember. I don't think I asked. Why?"

"Oh, I don't know. I'm just looking for pieces of the puzzle I guess, trying to fit them together."

"Yes, me too. I spent the afternoon trying to do just that, to read between the lines. But I don't think it's necessary."

"What do you mean?"

"I believe that what she said was what she wanted to say, what she wanted me to hear. There's no need for me to play detective. If she said she lived in that direction and nothing more, then that's all I have to know. You understand?"

"I think so, yes. But…"

"But what?"

"You're comfortable with that?"

"I am, yes."

"That's not like you."

"No, it isn't, you're right. I always want to know everything about everything, don't I?"

"Yes, you do. You're normally as curious as a child at a science fair – oh, what's that? How does that work? Explain it to me!"

"I know, it's an old habit. I feel like I've been set adrift on a raft or something if I can't get every question answered. But with this… I don't know how else to put it – I just have faith that things will go however they're supposed to go. The outcome, whatever it is, will be the right one."

Fr. Romero smiled. "Faith. Interesting choice of words."

That got a laugh from Fr. Fitz. "True. But that's exactly how it all began – not with questions, but with answers, with that feeling that I knew what I had to do. I didn't have to wrestle with it or figure it out, I only had to go where it led me, and it led me to her.

"It was like nothing I've ever experienced. She wasn't even in the same room as me when I first felt it, and yet I knew where she was and who she was. I hesitate to make the comparison, but the last time I felt so sure of anything, believed that strongly in a feeling… was when I was preparing to take my perpetual vows, and that took years. This was…" He snapped his finger in the air.

"Funny, you hit the nail right on the head. I've been thinking about exactly that – your vocation, and what this could mean to it."

"What do you mean?"

"Well, on some level I suppose it makes sense that she would approach a priest – there are theological implications that a priest might be best equipped to deal with. But by that same token it seems, I don't know, rather illogical. Her story, her very presence here flies in the face of what a priest believes, what he's been taught. So why choose him?"

"I'll put it another way - we deal with the natural all the time, and of course with the supernatural. But this is for lack of a better word, unnatural. So what does it do for you as a priest to become involved in this? That's what I'm wondering, and I just don't know."

"You're worried about me?"

"Yes, I am."

"Why?"

"Because whatever this is, it isn't only about her. It's about you, too. She could be here to give you something, but I'm more inclined to believe that something is going to be expected of you. You do see that as a possibility, don't you?"

Fr. Fitz could only nod. Then he reached out and touched Fr. Romero's hand. "Thank you, Paul, for your concern. And your honesty."

Fr. Romero sat up straight and smiled. "And thank you for trusting me enough to share this with me."

Fr. Fitz smiled. "Of course. So, tell me. How would you

advise me?"

He took a moment to consider his response. "Well, meet with her of course. Given the way you say it all began, the feelings you have, your certainty... what else can you do? I'll just say this - go into this as a priest first and a man second, do you follow me? You represent Christ on this earth at all times and that applies to this situation as well, all the more because it's so extraordinary."

"I understand."

Fr. Romero didn't seem so sure. "Don't be... up for grabs. Whatever you talk about tomorrow, I suppose you should try to take and not give. Perhaps there's something here which will benefit you as a priest, enhance your understanding and your faith. But if it turns out to be something which could alter it or diminish it... well, be on guard is what I mean to say, I guess."

"I will."

Fr. Romero looked like he had more to say, but his years as a priest had taught him other things, too – like how to recognize when it was time to change the subject. With a lighter voice he asked, "So, what time are you meeting her tomorrow?"

"Early. Before noon. The plan is just to spend some time together talking – about what, I don't know. I don't really think she does, either."

"It certainly sounds that way. Tell me, does she seem at all frightened?"

"Anything but. She's as cool as can be."

"Are you?"

"No. Not at all."

"Good, good. Well, I'm sure you'll both figure out what you're supposed to be doing as you go."

"That's what she said. It's my hope, too. We're meeting in

Central Park."

"Oh, the same place again?"

"No, on the west side. A place called Oak Bridge."

"Your idea?"

"Hers. She said it would be convenient, an easy place for us both to get to." Fr. Fitz smiled. "Frankly, I think she was just showing off her knowledge of the park."

"So you won't talk to her like a tourist again?"

"Precisely."

"You may be right. After all, she's come a long way to be a New Yorker."

Fr. Romero grew quiet for a moment. A question had been lingering in his mind and it almost escaped his lips - is she pretty? He wasn't sure why he would ask that. Maybe he was considering the effect it might have on his young friend if she was pretty. Maybe he was thinking about the effect it might have had on Jesus if this truly was someone he called a friend, spent time with.

There was no denying the fact that he was curious about her, but in the end he didn't ask it. Instead, he settled on something slightly different.

"What is it like to be around her?" He didn't think of it as a particularly loaded question. Even as he asked it he wasn't sure exactly what he meant by it or what sort of reply he expected. He certainly didn't expect complete silence, but that was what he got.

Fr. Fitz only stared off into the distance while he tried to come up with some kind of answer. He went over the events of the day in his mind, trying to remember what it felt like when he first sat beside her, when they were walking together, or when she laughed. It was all right there, he had forgotten nothing, but none of it seemed even remotely describable - it was either too personal or too fantastic, or both.

In the end he only raised his hands in a helpless gesture. "I really can't say," was all he could offer. A moment later he added, "Good. It feels good," and shrugged, disappointed that he couldn't do any better than that.

But Fr. Romero seemed to have no problem accepting that answer and moving on. "One more thing," he said. "Regarding the 'why you?' question - have you considered the connection between you and her?"

"What connection?"

"Your work, of course. You wrote about her in your latest book. You regularly speak about her in your appearances, don't you?"

"Well, yes and no. I talk about a number of women from the Bible, but as a group. I don't make a point of singling her out."

"No, but others do, don't they? I mean, some of the people you come up against try to co-opt her story, don't they? They even embellish it, try to inflate her stature and her place in history in order to promote their agenda."

"Yes, that's true."

"And in order to counter that you have to lower her stature in turn, don't you?"

"I try to correct the record."

"By cutting her image back down to size. In fact, you speak against her."

"Well, I wouldn't say that."

"No, but she might."

He thought about that. "You make it sound personal. I never really think of it like that."

"Again, she might. Just something to think about."

Fr. Fitz nodded. "I see your point. I'll keep that in mind, thank you."

Soon after that, Fr. Fitz said goodnight and headed up to his room. As he climbed the stairs he said a quick prayer that he might pass out as soon as his head hit the pillow, but he didn't expect it to be answered. It was a pretty safe bet that before he got any sleep he would first have to spend a few hours staring at the ceiling. Some of those hours would no doubt be devoted to thinking about the day he had just had, but some would have to be reserved for considering the warning his old friend had given him - be on guard.

That advice should have seemed reasonable enough, even obvious to someone who was always on guard, always defending his position. And it would have but for one thing – he simply didn't sense any danger. He understood why Fr. Romero felt there might be good reason to be worried, but he was honest when he said he felt no fear. Even that righteous feeling that appeared so naturally whenever he sensed opposition was nowhere to be found just then.

In truth, he found it exciting to be embracing a feeling of unsteadiness for once. This must be what it feels like he thought, to be adrift on a raft.

Saturday Morning

Fr. Fitz raised his hand to check the time. Still eleven twenty, same as it was the last time he looked. He rolled his eyes as he put his hand back down. He had probably looked at his watch a dozen times in as many minutes. It wasn't being late that concerned him but being early, which he was.

He couldn't help but feel anxious all morning. All he wanted from the moment he woke up was for eleven thirty to roll around. But he forced himself to read for a while and to watch some news, even though he found it nearly impossible to pay attention. He tried to busy himself any way he could so that he wouldn't leave the rectory too soon. If he did he might get to the park before Mary, and he didn't want that. He felt that not letting her arrive first would be impolite, somehow. He also thought it might look like he was doing reconnaissance, arriving ahead of her just to see how she got there or which direction she came from. He didn't want that, either. So, he kept himself busy and waited as long as he could before heading uptown.

And yet, despite all his efforts, when he stepped off the subway at seventy-second street he was almost thirty minutes early. He refused to even walk in the direction of the park until it was time, so for twenty minutes he had been strolling along Columbus Avenue admiring the pre-war architecture. That, and looking at his watch.

When he wasn't doing either of those things he was

thinking about his clothes. He couldn't remember a day when he had last given so much thought to what he was wearing. Of course, he didn't usually have to. Priests are like soldiers or police officers in that sense – the uniform fits any occasion. But he thought he might look more open-minded and relaxed if he wasn't all decked out in black, so when he got dressed that morning he put on a pair of jeans and a polo shirt – it was a Saturday, after all.

But at the last minute he had second thoughts. What if she was put off by how relaxed he looked? She had approached a priest, maybe she was expecting to see a priest. Looking too casual could be worse than looking too stiff. In the end he tried to split the difference. He changed into his customary black suit and clerical collar, but he put on a light blue shirt instead of the usual black or gray in order to soften his appearance.

By then he was having doubts about that choice too, but he was also growing tired of fretting over it, and he was beginning to doubt that his appearance would be as troublesome for Mary as it was for him. He figured that despite the blue shirt she would see a priest, and despite the black suit she would see a relaxed, open-minded man. Either way, she would have to take him as he was because he wouldn't be changing a third time.

He checked his watch once more a few minutes later, and was relieved to see that it was finally time to go. He turned and headed across seventy-seventh street, then crossed into the park. With each step he took along the path the more the commotion of the city faded into the distance, and the happier he was that Mary had chosen the park as the place to meet.

When he caught sight of her he was he was very pleased – in spite of himself he had managed to let her get there first, just as he wanted. She was easy to spot, even from a distance. While he was still on the path that wound down to the bridge he could see a number of people walking around, talking, and so on, but she was the only one standing still. In fact, she was the picture of calm, just leaning against the railing with her hands folded in front of her. He doubted he looked nearly that cool, even with his hands sunk deep into his pockets.

Once again he noticed the way she was dressed – another long skirt, another billowy blouse. No braid in her hair, but the overall effect was the same as the day before – earthy, hippie.

At exactly eleven thirty he stepped onto the bridge.

"Hello," he said as he drew up to where she was standing, about half-way across.

"Hello, Fitz," she said, her smile instantly in place.

He pointed to their surroundings. "I approve. Does this place have some significance for you?"

"No, none. I just like it. It's very beautiful, don't you think?"

He nodded. "Yes, I do."

After that, they stood together for some time quietly looking out over the lake, which was still except when the occasional row boat ventured that far north. He had assumed that speaking first was her job, but he soon began to feel that she was waiting for him to say something. He had to remind himself of what she said - she didn't have any more idea how or where to begin than he did.

"So," he said finally, "here we are."

"Here we are."

"What has it been, fifteen hours since I last saw you? Then it's been fifteen hours since I was able to think about anything else. I have so many questions. I'm sure you expected that."

"Yes."

"You don't mind?"

"No, I don't mind. I'll answer what I can."

She made no move to start walking anywhere, so he leaned on the railing beside her. There weren't quite as many people there as there had been at the hotel the day before, but they were far from alone. Still, if she was comfortable with it then he figured that was as good a place as any to begin.

"There's something I noticed yesterday, something about you, actually."

"About me?"

"Yes. You're here. That's a fact. We don't know why, but we both feel there's a reason, that your presence here is part of some plan, right? And it stands to reason that every part of this plan has been carefully thought out, you know, right down to the last detail. So when something doesn't seem to add up…"

"Like what?"

"Well, like your accent. You're speaking English, presumably for the first time, which must be even more mind-boggling for you than it is for me. But my point is, if you were meant to come to New York, to live here and speak to someone who lives here, then why do you sound like you're from Texas?"

She looked thoughtful for a moment. "Texas," she said to no one.

"Yes. Your accent is definitely southern, I'm guessing Texas. I thought maybe there was some reason for that, some meaning."

She only looked at him and shrugged.

"You mean, you weren't aware of it?"

She shook her head and laughed. "No."

He couldn't help looking puzzled. "Why do I find that so strange?"

"I don't know." She laughed again. "Well, is it a problem? I mean, are you able to understand me?"

"Perfectly."

She shrugged. "Well then." That seemed to answer that. She went on. "What else doesn't add up for you?"

"Well, please don't misunderstand me – I like your style very much, but is there a reason you dress the way you do?"

She looked down at herself. "How do I dress? Wait, don't tell me - like Texas?" He was glad to hear her joke. He had worried that these questions might offend her. Better that she found it all amusing. "Well, no, no not like Texas. It's more of a period thing, a style that was popular at a time when…"

"Yes?" She was watching him with an expression that said it probably didn't matter any more than her accent.

"Never mind," he said with a wave of his hand. "I was just wondering. It's not important."

"But you were hoping there might be some meaning to that, too?"

"I suppose so. I don't know."

"Well, what about you?" she said, pointing to his clothes.

"What, this?" he asked, touching his collar.

"Yes. Is there some meaning to the way you're dressed?"

"I always wear this. It's a symbol of my office. These are my work clothes, you might say."

"So you're working now? Is that what it means?"

It was his turn to laugh. It was amazing how she could zero right in on what he was thinking. With a sigh he admitted, "To be honest with you, I don't know what I'm doing now."

"Poor Fitz. You're getting lost in the details."

"Am I? I suppose so. It's very difficult not to."

"Oh, I know," she said. "I did it in the beginning, too. I mean, at first everything around me was new and different, even the very words I was speaking, as you pointed out. I had a head full of questions just like you do now – how, why, when? I wanted to understand everything that was happening just like you do now."

"But?"

"But then it dawned on me - understanding every little thing wasn't important. It was the big picture I needed to focus on."

"But the unanswered questions…"

"They'll stay unanswered. That's difficult for you, I know. It is for me too, especially when the little things don't feel so little. Put yourself in my shoes for a moment - I came here for only one reason, to see you. I've been here for weeks and I've known why the whole time, and yet I only came to you yesterday. You don't think I've puzzled over that, over what the reason was?"

"Did something happen? I mean, to keep you?"

"No, nothing happened."

"Maybe you just weren't ready for some reason."

"Maybe. Or maybe I was waiting for you to be ready. I really don't know. But that's what I mean, I can easily get caught up in asking all those questions - why, how, what happened - or I can accept that there are things I don't understand, maybe can't understand. In the end that's what I choose to do. I say that yesterday the time was right, and so I went to you. End of story."

"Then, I'm guessing you don't know how you knew where to find me either, how you knew that I would be at the hotel?"

Mary only shrugged. "No, I don't. And I won't let that question distract me, either.

"Another detail?"

"Yes, another detail that doesn't matter, because knowing how I found you or even how I got here won't help me understand why I'm here in the first place. It won't tell me what's supposed to happen now that we've met, and that's all that matters. That's all I want to know."

He nodded slowly. It was practical advice she was giving him. With only two more days to figure out why they met he couldn't afford to get too lost in wondering how.

"And we have only until tomorrow to figure that out, right?" he asked.

"I didn't know that until yesterday, not until I actually said it, but yes."

Fr. Fitz thought about that for a moment. "You had no idea? Not until yesterday?"

"No."

"But now you're certain."

"Yes."

"So things are still coming to you."

"Oh, yes."

"Me, too?"

"I assume so. After all, we're both in the same boat, asking why this is happening. I suppose answers could come to either of us. Why?"

He echoed her words under his breath, "Both in the same boat." For some reason the words made him think of what Fr. Romero had said the night before, about how they were connected. Suddenly he found himself wondering if there might be something to his words.

She could sense he was trying to work something out. When he didn't answer, she asked, "What is it?"

He hesitated another moment, not sure if it was important enough to bring up. "I wonder if…" he began finally.

"Yes?"

"Are you familiar with my work?"

She seemed to grow more serious at the mention of that. "Yes, I am," she said evenly.

"Really? The books I've written, the talks I give - all of that?"

"I know what you're referring to. Yes, I'm familiar with all of it."

He paused again, the sound of her voice making him wonder if he ought to drop it. It didn't seem like the most comfortable subject to raise, but at the same time he couldn't help feeling that he was on the right track, so he went ahead. "Do you have an opinion on it? Do you like it, dislike it…?"

She didn't answer right away. She seemed to need to think about it. Rather than wait for her, he went on. "The reason I'm asking is, I wonder if that might have something to do with why you're here."

She looked at him hard for a moment, then moved from her spot on the railing for the first time and stood facing him. "Do you feel that's something we should talk about? Is that what you're saying?"

He would have had no idea how to answer if she had asked him that question the day before. Even five minutes earlier he might have wondered if the subject was best avoided. But by then he was surprised to find that he was certain. "Yes. Yes, we should talk about it."

She studied him for a while longer before finally answering. "Okay, then we'll talk about it." And just like that it seemed, they were on a track. The right one, he hoped.

She started walking slowly across the bridge. After a few steps she stopped and looked over her shoulder, then tilted her head for him to follow. "Come on, let's walk," she said. Happily, he saw her smile had returned.

Saturday Afternoon

The next time Fr. Fitz checked his watch there was good reason - it was almost four o'clock. He held it up for Mary to see, amazed at how much time had passed.

They had been talking almost non-stop for most of the afternoon, but surprisingly little of it was about the business at hand. Despite the fact that they had a limited amount of time, neither of them felt overly-anxious about getting to 'it' once Fr. Fitz realized how they should begin. He thought that revelation would get them revved up, but it had the opposite effect. It reinforced the idea that things would happen exactly as they were supposed to. After that, neither of them felt the need to force anything. Instead, for those few hours they focused more on enjoying the day than on sticking to any agenda.

That's not to say they didn't try. They started out talking about his work as planned and they even came back to it now and again, but in between they drifted easily from one unrelated topic to another. They also let themselves be easily sidetracked, like when they came across a jazz band that was playing to a decent sized crowd by Bethesda Fountain. For almost an hour they sat on the grass, listening to one song after another while she questioned him about what they were playing and the kinds of music he liked to listen to.

At one point he noticed that she was looking at the statue atop the fountain.

"That's called The Angel of the Waters," he said, pointing to it. "It refers to a story in the Gospel of…"

She finished the sentence for him. "John." When he only stared at her, she said, "Chapter 5."

He didn't know whether or not he was supposed to be impressed that she knew that but he was, just like he was impressed that she knew so many other things. But he had more to say about the statue. On the off chance that he might know more than she did on the subject, he continued.

"Yes. The story is about an angel that blesses the…"

"The Pool of Bethesda. Yes, I know."

"Um, yes. Jesus healed a lame man there and…"

Mary leaned forward and put her hand on his. "I know what happened, Fitz. I was there."

She couldn't help but laugh at his expression – a mixture of surprise, confusion, and awe. But they didn't say anything more about it then. Surrounded by people as they were, that wasn't the best place to talk about such things, so they went back to listening to the music. She enjoyed it so much he could only manage to tear her away when the band finally took a break.

They stopped whenever there was something to watch or to admire, but otherwise they were on the move almost the whole time, covering most of the areas he was familiar with and then some.

Once he realized what time it was it occurred to him that the only thing they'd eaten all afternoon was a single pretzel, which they had shared. Buying it had led to one of the more funny – and awkward – moments of the day, when he asked a question which only got a laugh in response, "Do you… do you eat?" Yes, she ate and by then they agreed they were both hungry enough to eat a cow. They left the park in search of a place where they could do just that.

"Oh, this is perfect," Mary said as they entered a small pub a short while later, "I want the biggest burger they have."

When a waitress told them to sit anywhere they liked, Fr. Fitz led her directly to a table towards the back. She didn't know that he always did that, but she did notice that he made a point of choosing the chair that put his back to the room.

"You've been doing that all afternoon, you know."

"Doing what?"

"That. Turning your back to people. Every time we got near people you turned away from them. Are you hiding from someone?"

"Everyone," he said with a smile. He explained that it was an old habit - his clerical collar made him conspicuous, especially when he was trying to do something simple, like eat at a restaurant. At times, he explained it was like a magnet. People saw the collar and felt free to just walk up to you and start talking about whatever was on their minds, even if you were with other people, even if you were trying to enjoy a meal. It was a lot like being a celebrity.

"But with my back turned, I'm just another guy in a suit. See?"

"I see. But as a priest don't you want to feel, I don't know, accessible?"

"Yes, I do. Just not every minute of every day."

"Oh."

He was amazed at how selfish that sounded. "I'm sorry, that's not what I meant at all. Let me put it another way. Sometimes I need to be more focused than that. Right now I want to be accessible to just you. How's that?"

"Very nice. Thank you."

In spite of how relaxed the day had been up until that point, they knew it couldn't stay that way indefinitely. So it came as no real surprise to either of them when things began to change. After their waitress took their order and walked away neither of them spoke again. For the first time since they met on the bridge that morning they were silent.

Probably no more than a minute passed, but it was a long minute during which they simply looked at each other across the table. By the end of it he could see in her eyes what he knew she must have been able to see in his, too – we're close. He could sense that they were going to understand a lot more very soon, but not before they finally talked about his work.

Although Fr. Romero had referred to it as a connection between them, the few times they did touch on it during the day the only thing they learned was that they both held very strong opinions on almost everything he did, and it was never the same opinion. They had only managed to avoid getting tangled up in it by changing the subject often.

Fr. Fitz was surprised by that. He expected that once they realized where they should begin, things would get easier somehow, but it hadn't worked out that way. For the first time it was occurring to him that this wasn't necessarily supposed to be painless.

Apparently, Mary had the same idea. "I didn't think it would be this, something we disagree on."

"Is it a problem for you?"

She shook her head. "I can't say. I still don't know where we're going with it."

She was quiet for a moment. "But I want you to know," she said finally. "Your work is one thing, but I don't disagree with what's in your heart." She pointed to his chest as she leaned in closer to him and began reciting in a near-whisper, "'I believe in God, the Father Almighty, Creator of heaven and earth.'"

He was touched, and a little surprised that she knew the

Apostle's Creed. He smiled and picked up where she had left off. "'And in Jesus Christ, His only Son, our Lord.'"

"Exactly," she said.

"Why do you know that? And in the park, how did you about the Gospel story?"

"I know many things."

"Like what?"

"Like that. Like the Scriptures, like the history of your Church... many things."

He smiled. "The things that I know."

"Yes."

"I guess that makes sense. If we're expected to talk about these things, I mean."

"Yes. But, that doesn't mean..."

"That doesn't mean we see eye to eye on everything."

"Or anything at all. But that's just more details. Like I said, what you do is one thing. But what's in your heart, what makes you a good man... I would never do anything to take that from you. I hope you'll remember that."

He wasn't sure he understood exactly what she meant but he nodded anyway, expecting that he would in time. She meant him no harm. That much he already knew.

"Thank you," he said. Then he added, "You know, it's interesting that you say that – about what's in my heart. I'm used to being disagreed with. If people don't like something I've said or written they often tell me so, sometimes passionately. I welcome that, I really do. These are people with strong convictions. But there are others, people who just want to tear down my faith altogether, to go after what's in my heart, as you say."

"Why would anyone want to do that?"

He shrugged his shoulders. "I'm sure they have different reasons. I think most often it's to get back at the Church for something that happened or something they believed happened to them." He smiled. "Some try harder than others."

"Like what? Give me a 'for instance.'"

"Well, I was riding a crowded subway once and a woman just turned to me and began lecturing me on Papal misdeeds throughout history - Popes who had killed or who kept wives or mistresses, Popes who had made young boys into Cardinals... boys they liked very much... that sort of thing."

"Wow. Were you upset?"

"Upset? No. I remember being very impressed, actually - she knew all these names and dates right off the top of her head. She was very knowledgeable."

"You mean she was right?"

"Oh, absolutely. About everything. When she was done she just looked at me, waiting for my reaction."

"What did you do?"

"I said, 'I know.'"

"I'm sure that wasn't what she wanted to hear."

"Nope. That's what I mean – she wasn't just offering her own opinion about something, she didn't want me to agree with her any more than she wanted me to disagree. She just wanted me to be shocked and scandalized by what she said. She wanted to make me question everything I believed in by opening my eyes to the failings of my Church.

"The thing is, I know all about the failings of my Church. I know its history, good and bad. The kinds of things she was talking about, the selling of indulgences, and on and on... There's plenty there to be scandalized about, but none of it has anything to do with my beliefs.

"My goal is to serve the Church the best way I can, not to bemoan the mistakes of men that came before me, and certainly not to pretend that such things didn't happen."

She nodded at that, then asked, "Do you forgive people who try to hurt you like that? Did you forgive that woman, for instance?"

"Of course. And I felt for her. She was clearly hurting in some way." Then he added, "But she made me miss my stop. I didn't forgive her for that. I mean, it was rush hour…"

That got a slight smile. After that they didn't speak again for another minute, until he broke the silence rather clumsily. "I have no personal stake in any of it, you understand? I do what I do to promote the official position of the Church." He quickly added, "That's not an excuse, or a skirt I hide behind. They're my beliefs too. I just mean that I'm not on some sort of personal crusade."

"You may not have a personal stake in this, but I do." Her tone was much more serious now. "Maybe I'm the one who should be on a personal crusade."

"But, why?"

"Because I had a right to be remembered for the things I actually did, the contribution I made. Instead I'm known as the patroness of wayward women. The Penitent." She nearly spat the word out with disgust. "Mary Magdalene, the reformed prostitute, the forgiven adulteress, the washer of feet with her tears… for almost fourteen hundred years that was the official position of the Church. That's what was promoted.

"Of course, it worried no one than none of that was true, or even that there was no evidence for any of it in the Gospels. All it took was for your Pope Gregory to declare that nearly every woman named Mary in the Gospels was actually me, and some of the unnamed women, too. And just like that, all their stories were mine. All their sins were mine, too. Conflation – what a pretty word for such a dirty deed. Tell me, should I be happy with that?"

"No. No, you shouldn't. That never should have happened. It was a terrible injustice. What's more, it was bad theology. But they corrected the mistake more than forty years ago when the Second Vatican Council..."

"Corrected? Fitz, please. How exactly did they correct fourteen centuries of tradition – with an announcement read from the pulpits, an official apology of some kind? They did none of that. They simply separated my feast day from Mary of Bethany's feast day on their calendar. That was it.

"Who even knows about this 'correction' after forty years? Ask your parishioners who Mary Magdalene was. I can tell you exactly what they'll say - she was a whore, a sinner, the woman who Jesus saved from stoning. Not one of them can tell you anything about my story because it was written right out of your Good Book."

"I don't understand what you mean. You occupy a very important place in the Bible. St. Augustine said..."

"'The Holy Spirit made Magdalene the Apostle of the Apostles.'"

"Exactly. You're portrayed as beloved, brave, a devoted friend until the very end."

"Yes, a friend who was lucky enough to be in the right place at the right time once or twice, but who mostly just huddled together with a bunch of other women in the background. When she wasn't working as a prostitute, that is.

"Of course, it isn't necessary for that false depiction to continue to go unchallenged. There's more information available that could help people better understand the role I played. Some very important events were recorded in the Gospels of Thomas, Philip, Mary..."

Fr. Fitz began to shake his head.

"Apocrypha," Mary said with a smile.

"Yes."

"Exactly. Even when these Gospels resurface after being hidden away for so many years no one has a chance to learn anything more about me from them. The Church won't have anything to do with books that were excluded from the Canon."

"Excluded for good reasons."

"Some were good, others were not. My point is, the Church hasn't changed much in seventeen hundred years, has it? My story was suppressed from the start, then butchered, and now it's suppressed again."

He felt for her, and didn't want to simply challenge her point for point. "I understand how you must feel," he said.

She took a moment to make sure she was calm before continuing. "But you don't understand. I was respected in my time, Fitz, looked up to. For centuries I could have been an inspiration to others, to women. Instead my reputation was tarnished and I became a symbol to help keep 'uppity' women in their place.

I – the Penitent - was used to make countless generations of women into second-class citizens within their own religion, a religion that I helped create. Women were taught that like me they were sinners, dirty creatures by nature. Their only hope was to accept that and live a life of subservience. A few lucky women might be rewarded with nominal roles in the Church, but only as long as they remained quiet and didn't ask for too much.

"And I wasn't the only one. But you already know that, you're the historian. Any female contemporary of mine who refused to toe the line was simply edited into submission by jealous men once their pens hit the paper. Their 'position' was that women should be subservient, not equal, and that's the position of the Church you defend, to this day."

She paused, then she continued even more gently. "In my opinion a good man like you would do better to defend the position of Jesus himself, not the Church."

"But Mary, they're one in the same. The Church promotes the same Word Jesus was here to share with us. What I know of Jesus comes from the Gospels."

"The Gospels," she said with a sigh. "Remember who you're talking to. What I know of Jesus comes from Jesus himself."

She had to keep from smiling at the look that crossed his face when she said that - like a child being told he had missed the circus when it was in town. But he caught himself when she continued. "I'll trust my own memories over anyone else's account of what happened. Can you blame me?"

"No, I suppose not, but can you blame me? You must know my position on that subject."

"The Gospels were inspired?"

"Precisely. God's Word."

"All four?"

"Certainly all four, exactly as they are. To quote St. Irenaeus... 'Just as there are four regions of the world and four directions of the wind, so there are four pillars of the gospel God had given the world.'"

"And you buy that?"

"It does have a certain poetry."

"But Irenaeus was only rationalizing, responding to attempts to rid the Gospels of their contradictions. Marcion had already suggested that the Church should use only Luke's Gospel and ditch the other three. Tatian wanted what he called 'Gospel Harmony', for the four Gospels to be blended into one. Neither of those ideas sounds more reasonable to you?"

"It isn't for me to say what's reasonable. Whoever wrote the Gospels, however they were written… 'All Scripture is breathed out by God.' Timothy 3:16. I believe that, Mary."

"And when the Church decides to change that inspired Word?"

"Change? Like what?"

"In Exodus we were originally commanded not to covet our neighbors' slaves, but 'slaves' has somehow become 'servants.' How did God's own Word, His Inspired Word get changed? Did He breathe again, or is that simply the Church imposing political correctness on Him?"

"I see your point, but there have been several versions of the Gospels through the years. What you're referring to is just a different interpretation."

"Fitz, I realize you've been speaking English a lot longer than I have, but I don't believe that 'servant' is an interpretation of 'slave.' Changing that word reflects a complete shift in morality, not proofreading."

"Change, interpretation… either way, it's guided by the Church so it's still the Word of God. It isn't the same thing as embracing every new theory that comes along."

Something occurred to her when he said that. She felt she understood something more, something important. He could see it in her face even before she said anything. He didn't ask her what it was, didn't say anything. He only looked at her and waited.

When she spoke again it was in a very soft voice. "I'm not a new theory, I'm a fact. I knew Him, Fitz. And He knew me. I was there from the very beginning, part of everything He did." Then she added, "You wondered yesterday what was relevant." She tapped her finger on the table. "I believe this is… this is relevant."

"What? The Gospels?"

"Everything you call inspired." She put on her best school teacher voice. "'It is not from Sacred Scripture alone that the Church draws her certainty about everything which has been revealed. Therefore both sacred tradition and Sacred Scripture are to be accepted and venerated with the same sense of loyalty and reverence.'"

He opened his eyes in amazement. "You're quoting the Dei Verbum. So you think sacred tradition is relevant to this, too?"

"Probably even more so."

"Why more?"

"It's one thing to point to the Bible and say, 'This is where we get the authority to teach this lesson.' It's another when you can't even do that."

"But sometimes that's how it has to be. Not all God's teaching was written down. Some was passed down as sacred tradition from generation to generation."

"I could point out that all traditions are passed down that way, Fitz. So are recipes. So are bad habits. Jesus warned about that. He's quoted in Mark 7, saying, 'You have a fine way of setting aside the commands of God in order to observe your own traditions!'"

"Yes that's true, but that refers to man-made traditions. The recipes, as you say. Sacred traditions didn't come from men but from the Holy Spirit, through the apostles. They were the first to hand them down."

"I know your Church explains its belief in many things that way, things that aren't explicitly stated in the Gospels - purgatory, the perpetual virginity of Mary, the celibate priesthood, even the make-up of your Canon."

"Exactly."

"But unlike your Gospels these sacred traditions grow and change over time – like recipes. And since nothing is written down the Church's story simply changes along with them. But sometimes the stories don't quite work.

"Private confession to a priest is a perfect example. The story goes that the apostles were commanded to hear confessions and pardon sins, yet no apostle hears or offers a confession anywhere in the Gospels. Not once.

"And after they were gone? For six hundred years people confessed their private sins directly to God in prayer, just as Jesus instructed them to do. Six hundred years! Only then did a group of Celtic monks introduce the practice of private confessions to Europe. And it took another six hundred years for the sort of confession you hear today to become a regular practice.

"And yet, this somehow qualifies as a sacred tradition handed down by the apostles."

He continued to look at her questioningly, but still said nothing.

After a moment she smiled, then leaned forward and put her hand on his. "This is relevant," she said again. "Fitz, I'm still not sure what you're supposed to do, what you're supposed to get from all of this. But I know now what I'm supposed to do. I'm certain of it.

"I'm supposed to tell you about my life – before. Not just about me, but about the people I knew and how we lived. About Him. If you're going to speak for my friend Jesus, you should really know a little more about the man."

Saturday Evening

It was exciting to feel things coming more into focus, but the more they did, the more Fr. Fitz found he had to resist the urge to see design in every coincidence, or to look for meaning in even the smallest things, like their location.

They had been walking south along Central Park West since leaving the restaurant, when Mary suddenly said, "Let's sit here for a while," and took a seat half-way up a wide set of steps, invited him to sit beside her.

A smile crossed his face. He wondered if she realized they were on the steps of the Museum of Natural History. But he didn't bother searching for any meaning in that. He figured there was too much irony in their ending up in front of an evolutionist's paradise for there to be any significance to it.

He was going to make a joke about it, but he let it pass. He didn't want either of them distracted by that or anything else just then. He was thinking about what she said at the restaurant – that he should know more about Jesus. Something about that made him feel defensive, and he wanted to know exactly what she meant by it.

"First, tell me why," he said as he sat down beside her, "why would you be here to tell me about Jesus?"

"So you'll know, of course."

"But, I do know."

She only raised her eyebrows at that.

"Are you suggesting that I don't?"

"No, Fitz I'm not. But if you learned what you know about Him from the Gospels, then your knowledge is, let's just say, incomplete."

"Why do you say that?"

"Because it isn't all there. Inspired or not, there are huge gaps in the story. Many things were left out."

"If so, then that's how it should be."

"That's a historian speaking? Look at it this way, I'm not offering you anything different, just more, a chance to know more of the story. Are you telling me you don't want that?"

He didn't respond. He was genuinely unsure how he should feel about what was being offered to him. It occurred to him that her offer could be exactly what Fr. Romero had warned him to be on guard for. He was a priest, he had been educated for his job. Why should he need to know anything more? And what might it mean for him if he gained a deeper understanding, or got a fuller picture of the man behind the words and deeds he already knew so well? How might it change him? He simply didn't know, so he wasn't sure how to answer her.

Mary could sense his dilemma. "I told you," she said, reading his thoughts, "I'm not here to take away what's in your heart, your faith. Besides," she said with a sly smile, "I've come a long, long way for this. You wouldn't deny me the opportunity to fulfill my purpose, would you? You wouldn't be that ungallant."

After a moment he smiled. "No, I suppose I wouldn't," he said. He was catching up to her again, he could feel it. He knew there was more he could say but he also knew there was no point. She was right, this was what they were supposed to do.

He turned to face her a bit more. "Okay then, don't keep me in suspense any longer. Lay it on me. Tell me everything

I don't know about your friend."

She laughed at that. She seemed about to continue, but then she said, "Tomorrow. We'll do that tomorrow."

"Oh?"

She nodded. "I'm tired. Plus, I want you to have a chance to sleep on it. I want you to be absolutely sure that you want to hear what I have to say."

"I'm already sure, I think you know that. I'm supposed to hear what you have to say. But if you'd rather wait until tomorrow, that's fine. Only..."

"Hm?"

"Well, tomorrow is it. Will we have enough time for everything you want to tell me?"

"Yes, don't worry. We'll have plenty of time."

"Okay then, as you like."

She didn't answer. She only looked at him for a while, then started smiling.

"What?" he said.

She still said nothing, just smiled even more broadly. Soon he couldn't keep from smiling himself. "What?" he asked again. "What are you smiling about?"

"I'll share one thing with you now. Something I felt when I first became aware of you - at the very start, long before we even met. Something I felt again yesterday when I first heard your voice, and today, too. I felt it many times throughout the day today."

"What's that?"

"There are certain... parallels between you and Him."

"Parallels?"

"Similarities. I'm sure it's the reason I feel so comfortable with you. And maybe... maybe it's also why I waited so long to approach you, I don't know. But I'm sure it's no accident. I almost told you earlier, a few times."

He could hardly think of an appropriate response. True to form, he went for more information. "What similarities, if you don't mind me asking?"

"Anyone could see He was a good man, like you. He knew how to speak to people, of course. He had presence and could make Himself heard, just the way you can. Like you He wasn't afraid to cross swords with anyone, but He never looked for a fight, not ever. He truly enjoyed helping and caring for others, exactly what you do. Your strengths, like your intelligence, your humor, your ability to remain calm - those were His strengths, too."

Fr. Fitz was genuinely touched by the unexpected compliment. It isn't every day a person is compared favorably to the Son of God, even a priest. "Mary, I don't know what to say to that, I really don't."

She paused for a moment, then said, "There are other similarities, far more relevant ones, I think. But…"

"Tomorrow."

"Yes."

She's right, he thought. That was more than enough for one day. "All right, then," he said as he slapped his hands on his knees. He stood up, then gave her his hand to help her stand. As they walked together to the curb he asked, "Can I see you home?"

"After only our second date?"

He turned to see her laughing. "You should see your face," she said. "What's the matter, don't women ever joke like that with the crusading young priest?"

"Sure, all the time. But not old broads like you. They're usually a bit younger, like two thousand years."

She laughed again and he realized he liked the sound of it very much. She'll be gone in a day, he thought. I won't hear that laugh again after tomorrow.

"No, there's no need," she said. "I'll be fine. Thank you."

They made their plans for the following day, then he flagged down a taxi for her. As it pulled up she said, "Are you okay? You look a little lost."

"No, not lost. I'm just, you know… wound up. Too wound up to go right home, that's for sure."

"Well, it's still early. Why don't you go out, see a friend? Someone closer to your own age, maybe."

With that she said good night and got into the cab. He waved goodbye after closing the door behind her, then turned away. He wouldn't allow himself to see where the cab turned or which way they headed.

He hadn't exaggerated, he was far too wound up to even think about going right home. Plus, he didn't feel ready to face Fr. Romero, who would surely be waiting up for him. He would have a lot of questions and Fr. Fitz knew he wouldn't have any of the answers. There hadn't been enough time to process everything. He didn't know yet what to make of it all or even how to gauge where it was headed.

Maybe Mary had the right idea, he thought. Rather than dwell on it maybe he should call a friend. It wouldn't hurt to distract himself for a while, maybe even see a movie. Without thinking any more about it, he pulled out his cell phone and scrolled down the list of contact names until he came to Marianne's and then stopped.

The question entered his mind again - design or coincidence? This was Mary's suggestion, after all. Either way, he had to admit that Marianne was the perfect person to get in touch with. She was the one person he could envision himself actually talking to about all this someday. At the same time, she was probably the one person he could spend the evening with without feeling the need to bring it up at all. Plus – coincidence or not - she was in town.

But he hesitated before dialing. Not because of his feelings for her - considering everything else he was dealing with he felt confident that only her friendship would be on his mind if he saw her. Even being out one-on-one with a woman didn't concern him - they would just stay in very public places. But he worried that calling her could be awkward. In all the years he had known her he had only spoken to her by phone a few times, and never for anything but business.

He decided to text her instead. 'Hey, it's Fitz. Sorry, I know this is unusual. If you're free and feel like getting out call me.' Then he returned his phone to his pocket and continued walking south. If she called back, great. If not, at least he was heading in the right direction.

A thousand thoughts competed for his attention as he walked, but one managed to stand out above all the rest – it didn't matter how much he was on guard. He could not hope to pass through this experience and come out the other side unchanged. Already he was not the same man that he had been the day before, not by a long shot. And when he heard his phone ring he could only smile to himself and wonder who he was going to be the same time tomorrow.

Saturday Night

When he finally arrived back at the rectory Fr. Fitz was not at all surprised to find Fr. Romero asleep on a chair in the living room, an open book laying upside down in his lap. He considered tip-toeing by him and heading upstairs but that seemed even more rude than waking him up.

It didn't take much, just a tap on the shoulder. Fr. Romero blinked his eyes a couple of times and looked around as he leaned forward. "What time is it?"

"Not late. About eleven."

"Eleven is late." He looked at Fr. Fitz for a while. "And how are you?"

"I'm fine, fine."

"You just got in? That was a long day."

"Yes. I actually just came from seeing a movie."

"A movie? Really? I wonder if she and Our Lord were big movie goers."

"Probably not. Besides, I wasn't with her. I left her a while ago. I went to the movie with a friend to clear my head."

"I see." He sniffed the air. "I like your friend's perfume." Fr. Fitz only smiled at that.

"Paul, I'm sure you're curious but I don't have much to say, really. I'm sorry. I need to think about it a while first."

"I thought you might. That's fine. Tell me, are you seeing her again tomorrow?"

"Yes, in the morning. Then that's it – that's the third day."

Fr. Romero nodded. "Well, you'd better get to bed then. Me, too." He got to his feet and started walking with Fr. Fitz towards the stairs.

"How was the movie?"

"Terrible. A waste of time." That might have been true, he didn't really know. He could barely remember the name of the movie he saw, let alone anything about it. He and Marianne didn't really care what they were going to see. She was as anxious to get out of her hotel room as he was to get out, period. They bought tickets to the first thing they found playing, then sat through the first hour of it talking and paying no attention whatsoever before finally leaving to get some dinner.

He had never before seen her twice in two days outside of work, and he was not at all surprised to find how happy it made him feel. As he had hoped, he was never once tempted to bring up what had been going on the past couple of days. Once he was in her company, it was easy to put those thoughts aside for a while. And when it was time to tell her everything, he knew that would be easy, too.

When they reached the top of the stairs Fr. Fitz said good night to his friend and headed to his room, exhausted. As he lay in bed he tried to bring it all back to mind, to replay everything that had happened that day, but he had no luck. All he could really think about was what would happen tomorrow. He managed to do very little of that either before drifting off to sleep.

Sunday Morning

The next morning didn't begin at all the way Fr. Fitz thought it would. It was their last day after all, time was short. He fully expected them to feel more of a sense of urgency than they had the day before and to get right down to business. Instead the morning's first order of business turned out to be clothes again. And laughter.

He was laughing out of disbelief as much as anything. When he finally caught his breath he pointed at her. "Is this because of me? Because of what I said?"

She looked like a completely different woman, dressed in white jeans, a peach top, and flat shoes. Even her hair was different, tied up in a pony tail. The only thing that remained the same was her smile.

"Well, you said I looked like a hippie."

"I didn't think you knew what that was."

"I didn't. I learned. So what do you think? Do I still look like one?"

"Man, oh man. No, you don't look at all like a hippie... which was not a bad thing, by the way." He found it sweet that she should have cared enough about his opinion to go to the trouble of changing her appearance for him. And he was not one to miss a cue. "If you don't mind me saying, you look very beautiful."

"Thank you very much," she said. "And you!"

He looked down at the jeans he didn't change back out of

that morning. "Yeah, for once I'm not the man in black."

She pointed to the neck of his t-shirt. "And you're not wearing your collar."

"No. I didn't want to have to turn my back to people, as you say."

"So, you're in disguise, is that it?"

"Not at all. This time I'm properly dressed to devote my time to you."

She nodded at that. "Good, I'm glad."

He looked past her and pointed. "So, this is the scene of the crime for today, huh?" They were standing outside the Metropolitan Museum of Art. Once again, her idea.

"Yes, this is it. I…"

She stopped in mid-sentence when a passing car caught her attention. Its windows were open and she could hear 'Across the Universe' playing loud on the radio. She pointed after it. "I've heard that music before. A few days ago."

"That? That's the Beatles."

She stood watching the car, looking wistfully after it as it disappeared down Fifth Avenue and the sound of the music grew fainter. "I like it very much," she said after she could no longer hear it. She looked sad to have lost it, maybe even sad that she might never hear it again. For all he knew, that was exactly the case.

Not for the first time he wondered what came after this for her. Three days with him, and then what? Back to her big girl apartment on the west side hardly seemed the likely answer. He could only guess at what the whole experience had been like for her since she hadn't said much of anything to him about it. How many wonderful things had she discovered in those few short weeks? How many wonderful things was she preparing to give up? He couldn't even begin to imagine. More than a song, he was sure of that.

"If you had more time," he said, "I could introduce you to a lot of music. To many things."

Her face brightened as she turned to him. "Maybe next time."

That almost wasn't funny, but they both smiled anyway.

"Come on," she said, "Let me show you around the place."

Mary Magdalene, he thought as they entered the main hall, my New York tour guide. It was not the easiest idea to digest.

He was about to ask her, "Was there something in particular you wanted to see, or are we just going to walk around a bit?" But he didn't bother. He already had the feeling that she was leading and he was following, and that was enough.

They walked quietly until she stopped to get a drink of water at a fountain. Then she picked up more or less where they had left off outside. "I used to enjoy listening to music," she said suddenly. "We all did."

"Oh?"

"Yes, very much," she said. "Whenever we could."

"Really?"

"Sure, why not?"

"Oh, I don't know. I don't recall ever reading anything about it."

"You mean in your Gospels?"

He laughed at that dig. "I mean, there's the story of the wedding of course, but even then I don't think there's any mention made of the music in particular."

"The wedding? You mean Cana?"

He nodded.

"Well, that was one, yes. But it was hardly the only one. This is what I meant by 'incomplete.' Many of our friends were young, Fitz. Naturally we went to many weddings."

"Naturally," he said, having never even considered the idea before. "And you enjoyed the music?"

"Mm, hm."

"Did you dance?"

"Of course we danced. We weren't Essenes." She laughed at her own joke. "Dancing was a big part of every wedding celebration, just like it is now."

"And He... He danced, too?"

She laughed even harder at that. "Not very well."

"What?!"

"He was a man, Fitz. He was gifted at some things, not so much at others. But to answer your question, yes He danced when there was music. He also laughed and smiled when He was happy, which was often. He ate when He was hungry and He drank when He was thirsty. He did all the things everybody else did. He was a man." She waited before continuing. "Does that surprise you?"

"It shouldn't, I guess. But there's an image that most people have of Him that's rather, I don't know, flat. You know - a very serious man, travelling from town to town healing and preaching twenty-four hours a day. He hardly ever stopped to eat or sleep, and He certainly had no time for things like dancing and laughing."

She shook her head. "And is that the image you have of Him, too?"

He shrugged his shoulders. "I don't know. I never envisioned him dancing, I can tell you that." He smiled. "It's hard to. We're taught to see Him a certain way from early on, I guess. For instance, I can remember being told by one of my nuns when I was just a boy that we never read of Him laughing in the Gospels, and so therefore we know that He never laughed."

"Oh, my. And did you believe that?"

He shrugged again. "Well no, I suppose I didn't. At least, I never wanted to. I always kind of felt sorry for Him, you might say. I thought, now here's a guy doing important work, making lots of sacrifices – He's entitled to a break now and again. I always hoped that He laughed a great deal, to be honest."

"Like you do."

He smiled. "Like I do."

When they reached the main staircase she motioned for him to go up. After a few steps she continued. "I'll tell you something Fitz, you're exactly right. I've seen many pictures of Him lately – here in the museum, in churches, in books, all over. These artists must have been taught by the same nun who told you He never laughed – they've got it wrong, all of them. They all make Him look gloomy and distant. Even in the few pictures where He's smiling He seems to be a thousand miles away.

"Yes, He was a serious man, very focused, very thoughtful, but He was not a thousand miles away. He was present and He was full of life. He smiled easily and He talked a lot and He most certainly laughed. He was engaging, do you understand? Not apart from us."

She paused for a moment. She seemed to be thinking about something else. "Later, He became much more serious, of course. There wasn't much to laugh about once He knew what would happen…"

She took the next few steps in silence, then suddenly stopped and turned to him. "What happened to Him later… I'm sorry if you have questions about that, but it's not something I want to talk about."

"Of course," Fr. Fitz replied, "That's fine."

"Like I told you, these things may have happened a long time ago, but I can still feel them. I can feel the loss…"

"I understand. To be honest, I don't want to talk about it, either. I don't think it's even relevant."

She seemed to appreciate him saying that. "No, I'm sure it isn't."

With that they continued climbing the stairs. "This way," she said when they reached the top. She guided him to a gallery at the end of a long corridor and came to a stop in front of a large painting of a young woman. She was sitting in front of a mirror, holding a skull in her lap and looking off into the distance – at something or away from something, he couldn't tell. But he recognized the symbolism right away.

Mary pointed to the label beside it. "Read that."

He leaned closer and began to read to himself. She smacked him lightly on his arm. "To me. Out loud."

"Oh, I'm sorry. It says 'The Penitent Magdalen by Georges de La Tour.'" He stood up straight to look at the painting again. "Well, it's not a very good likeness, is it? Except for the hair, maybe."

"Stop joking. Keep reading."

"Okay, let's see. 'A sinner, perhaps a courtesan, Mary Magdalen was a witness of Christ who renounced the pleasures of the flesh for a life of penance and contemplation. She is shown with a mirror, symbol of vanity; a skull, emblem of mortality; and a...'"

She cut him off. "That's enough." She studied the painting herself for a moment, then sighed. "How many of these have you seen, do you think?"

"What do you mean?"

"Paintings like this – these 'Mary Magdalene the repentant sinner' paintings. How many have you seen?"

He shook his head. "Oh, I don't know. Many."

"Mm, hm. They're not hard to find, the Church commissioned a lot of them through the years. They're hanging on the walls of museums and art galleries all over the world, even in the Churches themselves. They help teach each new generation the same old tired stories and keep them from learning anything new about me. As propaganda, they're very effective."

When he didn't respond she asked him, "You don't see it that way?"

"As propaganda? I don't know. I don't know how deliberate it all was or is. But they do have the effect you're talking about, there's no denying that. They keep a very unflattering picture of you alive. I'm sorry."

"I'm sorry too, Fitz. For you. This affects you more than it does me."

"Me? Why do you say that?"

"Because the Church used to use these artists to perpetuate these lies, but these days they have something far better. They have you."

He walked around her and leaned up against the wall but didn't say anything right away. He knew there was no point in giving knee-jerk answers in defense of the Church. After all, it wasn't really the Church she wanted to talk about, but him. By then, he knew that. By then he was starting to know much more.

"You said you wanted to tell me about your life," he finally said.

She nodded.

"But it's not just this, is it? It's not a question of a bad reputation. There's something else you want to tell me, isn't there?"

She didn't answer, so he kept going. "And it's supposed to change something, isn't it?" After a moment he said, "Me. It's supposed to change me."

"I don't know," she said. "I really don't. I only know what

I'm supposed to do, not what comes after that."

"But you're holding back, I can tell. Why?"

He smiled when a look of concern came over her.

"Please don't worry about me," he said. "I'm secure in what I know, and in what I believe."

"I know you are."

"Like I told you, I'm ready to listen to you." He took her hand and gave it a squeeze. "Whatever it is, just tell me. I'll deal with it, or try to understand it, or reject it, or whatever I feel I have to do."

She was glad to hear him sound so certain. She also knew he was right - it was time that she told him what she had only hinted at up until then. For all she knew, he already had some idea where she was headed anyway. "Okay. Just one more stop first," she said.

She led him to another gallery, walking a bit faster this time. Again she steered him to a large painting and repeated the exercise, asking him to read the label.

"'The Penitent Magdalen by Corrado Giaquinto.'" This time he didn't need to be told to keep going. "'According to the Golden Legend, Mary Magdalen ended her life in a cave near Marseilles where she was visited daily by angels...'"

He didn't bother finishing it. Neither of them needed to hear the penitent part that followed.

By that point he felt he could ask her anything at all. "You said the other day you didn't remember where you ended up. Do you now? Could it have been in Marseilles, as the story says? Did you... did you die there?"

She shook her head slowly. "I know I travelled, but I really don't know where I settled down, or even if I did. I know that must sound odd to you, that I can remember certain things very clearly and others not at all, but that's just how it is. As for dying..." She shrugged. "There was that time, now there's this. How one ended and the other began…" She held up her hands in a futile gesture. "Your guess is as good as mine."

"Actually, there's more to some of those stories." He spoke the next words more softly. "Some say you left Jerusalem pregnant… with His child."

She seemed to have no trouble remembering that. She shook her head quickly. "No."

Before Fr. Fitz could respond he felt a tap on his shoulder, and turned to see two elderly priests standing behind him. It might have been because of what he and Mary were talking about or because he was dressed in civilian clothes, but for whatever reason the sight of them made him feel like a schoolboy who'd been caught playing hooky.

But they weren't there to bust him, just to look. One of the priests pointed past him and asked in a heavy Spanish accent, "Would you excuse me, please?" With a quick apology he and Mary moved from in front of the painting they were blocking. They watched as the priests looked over the painting, then made a few comments back and forth in Spanish before moving on to the next one.

When the priests had moved far enough away Fr. Fitz asked her, "What did they say about it?"

"How would I know?"

"You don't speak Spanish?"

Mary raised her eyebrows. "I don't even know how I'm speaking English."

He laughed at that, not all sure if she was trying to be funny. Then a thought occurred to him. Nodding towards the two priests he asked her, "What would He make of it all, do you think? What would He think of the Church and what we've done in His name after all these years?" He may not have known what kind of answer he expected to that question, but he was sure that what she came back with wasn't it. "He wouldn't recognize it, honestly. But there are some things about it that would please Him."

He waited, hoping she might explain what she meant by that, but when she didn't say anything more he asked, "He wouldn't recognize it? What do you mean? Why not?"

She looked surprised by his question. "Do you honestly think your Church bears any resemblance to anything that existed in our day? Fitz, just how many churches do you think He built? How many grand cathedrals? He didn't guard His message jealously, he made no one come to Him in order to hear it. He preached freely in people's homes, outdoors… wherever they were gathered.

And when we walked into a town, Fitz you couldn't tell us from just another group of locals. You couldn't tell Him from any other man in our group, for that matter. Your Bishops today need to dress up in their purple cassocks and their finery in order to command attention, but He didn't. He did it with no costume, no uniform.

"And there was a reason for that, Fitz, which seems to have gotten lost somewhere along the way. He didn't want to be set apart. He wanted to be on par with the people his message was intended for, one of them, so that both He and His message would be accepted.

"That went for his actions, too. He served in the trenches just like the rest of us. First among equals maybe, but equal. But today even that has been turned up-side down – your Church leaders are pampered, and venerated. They live in castles with servants to tend to them. And the people they're supposed to be serving are serving them instead, kissing their rings and bowing when they pass, treating them like royalty.

"Well, He needed none of that and He wouldn't

understand why they do. His message was all He had to make Him stand out, and it was enough. It should still be enough."

"But it's not the same now, what we're doing is not the same. No one can reach a world-wide audience the same way He reached out from town to town in the beginning. It requires a different way of doing things."

"That's your Church speaking in a nutshell. Even while they claim to be carrying on His work they point out how much they've moved away from it. Believe me, your Church hasn't changed because it's grown, but because it's teaching a different message now.

"His lessons were always simple... God exists in each of us, so we don't have to pay or go through intermediaries in order to find Him. We can confess our sins directly to Him, and ask for His forgiveness. We can thank Him for our blessings or ask Him for help all on our own. And because God is in each of us, a Father to all of us, no one is better or worse than anyone else, regardless of wealth or position.

"That's how He taught. And he did it by daily example. Do your Church leaders spend their days among the sickest and the worst sinners the way Jesus and His followers did? Is that the example they set?

"No, your Church as it exists today was not created by Him, but by men. He would not recognize it."

Fr. Fitz didn't respond at first, there was a lot to think about in what she said. But he nodded his head finally and said, "We're not perfect, I know. As human beings we priests have our faults..."

"We all have faults, Fitz. No one knew that better than He did, and no one forgave them faster. But I was referring to what he would think of the Church, not individual priests. As much as it has changed, your Church is still supposed to be continuing His work."

"And you're saying it doesn't?"

"It does sometimes. And sometimes it contradicts Him by not following His teaching."

"When?"

"I'll give you an example. I went to visit a Church the other day, right here in the city. It was very pretty, and it had a brand new walkway made of bright red bricks out front.

"The bricks caught my attention because they had dark stripes on them, or so I thought. But when I looked closer do you know what the stripes actually were? Names. The names of all the people who had donated money to pay for the walkway were engraved into the bricks.

"Standing there I couldn't help thinking of a verse right from one of your Gospels - I'm sure you know the one I mean... 'So when you give to the needy, do not announce it with trumpets, as the hypocrites do in the synagogues and on the streets, to be honored by men. I tell you the truth, they have received their reward in full.'"

"Matthew 6:16."

"Exactly. Well, He considered that a very important lesson. I heard Him say it on more than one occasion. But is it being taught? Well, at that particular Church they want the money for a new walkway so bad they actually encourage people to boast publicly about their generosity. They even provide the bricks.

"That's just one Church, I know. But there are many more with similar things - donor recognition walls, plaques... you name it. That's not continuing His work. That's trying to serve both God and money, with money coming out on top."

Fr. Fitz nodded slowly. "Well, I certainly won't give you any argument there. I'm sure it would sadden Him to know just how often priests are so busy being administrators that they miss opportunities to teach simple lessons. I don't imagine He was ever too focused on raising money."

"We didn't build many walkways, no."

They were quiet for a moment, then Fr. Fitz said, "You said there are things that would please Him."

"Yes. When He envisioned a class of teachers to come after Him, He saw more that were just like us, the way we were." Mary paused, then said, "Like you. He would be very pleased with you. A good man who spends his time caring for others. A man who isn't afraid to go out into the world and spread the Word. A man who isn't interested in the trappings of his office. You and all the others like you He would be very pleased with."

Fr. Fitz smiled. Her compliment was touching, but it wasn't that he was smiling about. "So we're finally there," he said. "'Just like us.' Those were your words. Or, did you think that escaped me, that I didn't hear you?"

"I know you heard me. You always hear me. Just like He did."

"So, now what?"

Mary took his arm and began leading him out of the gallery. "Now I tell you a bit about me."

Sunday Afternoon

It didn't surprise him that they would end up on the balcony over the Great Hall. It was a spot he liked to come to sometimes just to watch the throngs of people coming and going below. It was one of those rare places where he found it easy to be the viewer and not the viewed. He figured she knew that. Even with all the things she didn't know or couldn't remember she always seemed to know what was important to him - like for instance, the fact that he was ready. And once she was sure of it she simply started right in.

"I'll give you another quote - Deuteronomy 4:2. 'Do not add to what I command you and do not subtract from it, but keep the commands of the Lord your God that I give you.'"

He nodded.

"But that isn't what happened. I mentioned Tatian yesterday, his idea to combine the four Gospels into one, his 'Gospel Harmony'. Your Church rejected that in favor of keeping the four Gospels as they are."

"Yes."

"But they did it, anyway. They may have kept the four stories intact, but what they teach is actually a single story, a combination of all four. There's all kinds of adding going on."

"You're going to give me an example of what you mean?"

"I'm going to give you several. Take Judas' death.

Matthew says Judas hanged himself, but he doesn't say where or how. Acts says Judas first bought himself a field, then fell there and burst open in the middle. Those are two completely different stories with nothing in common. So how does your Church handle that obvious contradiction? Does it choose one story over the other? No, it combines them. They say Judas did indeed buy that field and that's where he hanged himself from a tree. Days later his body fell to the ground, bloated from hanging out in the sun, and burst open.

"Now, that's a very neat story. The only problem is that it doesn't appear anywhere in the Gospels. There isn't any mention of a tree in either story, no mention of time passing between his death and the bursting open, and yet that's what's taught. I would call that adding, wouldn't you?"

Fr. Fitz nodded slowly, but didn't say anything.

"Your Church doesn't. They say there was nothing to add or combine because there was no discrepancy between the stories to begin with. According to them each writer was simply reporting on a different aspect of the same incident – one focused on the hanging, and the other focused on the part about him bursting open. Personally I find that explanation remarkable.

"I'll give you an even better example. The names of Jesus' apostles are listed in Matthew, Mark, and Luke, but each list is different. Thaddaeus appears in one, Lebbaeus in another, and Judas, Son of James in the third. Are these three different men? Your Church says no, it's the same man who for some reason went by three different names, so it combined the three stories and he's now referred to as Judas/Thaddeus/Lebbaeus.

"And what do the Gospels say about the apostles' marital status? Paul clearly states that they were all married to

93

'believing wives' in Corinthians, and yet the Church regards them all as unmarried except for Peter.

She smiled. "You know why the Church admits that Peter was married, of course."

"Because it says in Matthew that Jesus treated his mother-in-law, who was sick."

She nodded. "That would seem pretty solid evidence, don't you think? But do you know what I heard suggested the other day? That's only proof that Peter HAD BEEN married. Peter's wife had probably died by that time that Jesus found him.

"I'd call that last bit adding – it appears nowhere in the Gospels. But it does serve the Church as justification for imposing celibacy on its priests.

"But, this is my favorite of all. Luke – and only Luke – states that Jesus sent out an additional seventy disciples to preach His message and heal the sick in different towns. Or was it seventy-two? Well, either way it's clear that His brother James was first among that group. Or, maybe not. His brothers Jude, Joses and Simon may have been among them, too. It all depends on which list you come across, because there are several.

"And of course, I'm only calling these men His brothers because the Gospels call them that - the inspired Gospels which also say that He had sisters. But somehow that is still debated. Some claim that He had no siblings at all, only step-siblings. It all depends on whether or not Joseph was married before, or if he and Mary had 'relations' before Jesus was born, or if Jesus was close enough to His cousins to call them brothers…

"Inspired or not, it all still seems to depend on who you ask, doesn't it?"

Fr. Fitz couldn't help himself. "Has anyone ever told you

that you have a way of really making a point?"

She smiled, but she wasn't finished. "Okay, enough examples. All I'm saying is that in spite of all its supposed regard for four different Gospels, your Church still manages to craft a single story out of them – whatever combination of stories suits it best, that's what they teach."

"And yet! When it comes to women they do exactly the opposite. They take what little information there is and use it to create no story at all.

"Take that second list of disciples – seventy, seventy-two... the number makes no difference. What matters is that you can't consider it at all unless you're willing to concede that there were women among those numbers. And there were. Many of them were even named on the lists, like Tabitha. And Priscilla, who was there with Aquila. Most importantly there was Junia, who was there with Andronicus.

"In Romans Paul says that Junia and Andronicus were of note among the apostles. Apostles, he called them both. But despite that, many in the Church refuse to accept that a woman was handpicked by Jesus to be a missionary. To get around Paul's words they've argued for centuries that Andronicus' partner was not actually a woman named Junia, but a man named Junias.

"And the rest of the women in that group? The Church says they went along simply as helpers, probably to cook and sew for the men. They did not preach or heal the sick on their own. There is no proof of that whatsoever, but they teach it any way. That's not adding or subtracting, it's fabrication.

"Well, let me tell you... there were many women in that group – preachers and healers, all of them." She pointed to herself. "Like me. He handpicked me to go out among them, too, Fitz. Me."

She waited before continuing. "Does any of that surprise you?"

He raised his eyebrows. "No. I suppose it doesn't. I know it should, but... " He didn't really know what else to say.

"Not since those four Gospels were first settled upon has your Church been able to make up its mind about a whole host of pesky little details that don't jive from one to the next - who Jesus actually claimed to be, what His true nature was, the meaning of His message and whether it was for Gentiles or Jews alone... You know, the little things. But when it came to the role of women in the Church they were never in doubt. There would be no role."

She paused to let him collect his thoughts. After a moment he asked, "But if you – women, I mean - were that involved, how was it not known at the time?"

"It was. It was known and accepted, but not by everyone. After He was gone... others were left in charge, and some of them thought differently about working beside women. In that sense it was just like it is today.

"We became marginalized. It wasn't doo difficult, really. We were sent mostly to places where we wouldn't find a kind reception, where there was little for us to do. Naturally we had less and less success, and we became less and less important. Then, when the stories were written we just weren't included. Like I said, it doesn't make the Gospels wrong, just incomplete."

He was watching her closely, and when she didn't continue, he said, "There's more, isn't there?"

"Yes. Something about Him, and also about you. I told you there were other similarities."

He didn't even have to be told. "I know. He loved you."

Tears came to her eyes. "Yes."

"But you were never together."

"No."

"Why?"

"There were so many people competing for his attention all the time, for His affection and His trust. He thought if it looked like he was favoring me…"

"You wouldn't be respected."

She nodded. "But I loved Him. And He loved me. Like you love her."

"Marianne?" It no longer surprised him what she knew.

"Yes. You love her but your work keeps you apart from her. Same thing."

And that was where it ended, more or less. After having delivered so much in such a short amount of time, she was suddenly very quiet. She turned and looked out over the railing.

"Do you need to sit down?" he asked.

"No, I'm alright, thank you. The thing is, we loved each other," she said again, "but we chose to remain apart so that my reputation would not be questioned. Would you say we made a good choice? Two thousand years later you can find my portrait hanging in museums all around the world, immortalized not as a respected teacher, but as the penitent whore. We gave everything up… for that."

He wasn't sure what he could say to that for her sake or his own, so he stayed quiet. But he choked back the feeling that it would an inappropriate thing to do, and put his arm around her shoulders.

She went on. "I brought His message to so many people. I understood it and Him better than anyone else. And today that wouldn't even qualify me to teach Sunday school. I would first have to forget everything I know and memorize all the trite little tales you've distilled his message down to."

He gave her shoulder a squeeze. "Oh, I don't know. Personally, I wouldn't hire you even then."

She leaned her head against him and let out a deep sigh. "Okay," she said. "I've said what I had to say. Now buy me lunch."

Sunday Evening

Neither of them had said a word in nearly a half hour. From where they sat on the grass behind the museum they could see so much activity - people walking, people running, people talking, fighting, playing, singing - there hardly seemed to be any need for them to do anything but sit and watch.

They were sharing their second pretzel in two days. Again, he could have made a joke - she ate three-quarters of it – again, he let it pass. But when it was gone she turned to face him.

"You've been a terrific host, Fitz."

He sat upright. "What? Now? Wait, Mary, I…"

"No, there's no need to say anything more. We're done. I have a good feeling about what I did. I believe I got it right. Whatever comes next for you, if anything… well, that's for you to feel good about."

She looked off across the park, towards 'home'. "It's time for me to go," she said.

He took her hand. "I don't know how to tell you… to tell you how much…" He gave up and laughed. "Like I said, I don't know how." Then he held up a finger and said, "Wait, wait, I do know. Don't get up yet."

He took out his phone, pressed a few buttons and slid over beside her. Mary's eyes suddenly opened wide as Across the Universe began playing. He leaned in close and held his phone up between their ears so they could both hear it.

She stayed perfectly still while she listened. She didn't speak, barely even seemed to be breathing. There was a trace of smile on her face that didn't change the whole time. When it was done she turned to him and said, "Thank you, Fitz. Thank you very much."

"You're welcome." Then he added, "Can I see you home? Can I walk you?"

She gave him a slight smile. "Not where I'm going." With that she stood up, motioning for him to stay where he was. She took the first few steps backwards. "You're a good man, Fitz," she said. Then she turned and began walking across the park.

He felt the loss of her immediately, as he knew he would. It became harder with each step she took, but still he didn't take his eyes off her until she disappeared behind a small hill, and then she was gone.

Monday Morning

About an hour before the conference was scheduled to begin Fr. Fitz walked through the front door of the hotel. Trying to keep his head down he walked quickly across the lobby and pushed his way into the first elevator with an open door. Had anyone seen him? He had the vague feeling that someone had tried to get his attention as he raced on by but he couldn't be sure. In truth, he really didn't care.

He almost didn't make it to the hotel at all. He very nearly listened to the part of himself that was screaming for him to bolt – jump in a car, get on a plane, anything, but get the hell out of there. He passed the third floor where the auditorium was located and continued straight up to the sixth floor where Marianne was staying. Moments later he was standing in front of the door to her room, hoping she was still there. After taking a deep breath he knocked three times, hard.

"Fitz!" she exclaimed when she opened the door, her face bright. She looked up and down the hallway, then winked at him suggestively. "Fitz, a movie is one thing but coming to my room? I mean, what will people say?"

When he didn't respond she looked at him more closely. Only then did she notice how troubled he looked. "Fitz? What is it? What's wrong?" She pointed to the simple shirt he was wearing. "You're not even dressed. What's the matter?"

"Can I come in?"

Rather than answer she simply took him by the hand and led him into the room. She sat him on the bed and took a seat in the chair opposite him. "Do you want some coffee, or some water or something?" she asked him.

"No, nothing. Thank you."

She raised her eyebrows and held up her hands, asking what? He took her hands in his and looked into her eyes, searching for the understanding he had always found there, the understanding he so desperately needed at that moment.

"Marianne... I can't do this. I can't be part of this conference."

"What? Why not?"

He kept trying, as he had been doing all the previous night and all that morning to find some way to begin, some way to work up to what he had to say, but he found nothing. Finally, he just shook his head and sighed.

"I've just spent three days with Mary Magdalene."

Two Years Later

Becca sat with her purse on her lap and her overstuffed carry-on bag on the seat beside her. On top of her purse was her lap-top, which she was typing away on. She was an experienced traveler and a good one. Any seat, anywhere could be her office, even a busy airport terminal.

"You know Fr. Fitz..." She stopped and laughed. "I'm sorry, I did it again. It still seems natural to call you that."

"Don't worry," he said, "I'm sure I'll be answering to that for many years yet. I'm far more used to it than you are."

In fact, he no longer was Fr. Fitz. Even though he hadn't been for more than eighteen months, he understood how easily people could forget. Even he did, from time to time.

Coming to the decision to leave the priesthood had not been difficult for him - it was a foregone conclusion. His beliefs were no longer the same as the Church's since he now embraced ideas that conflicted with what they and he had been preaching for years.

Technically, of course, he was still a priest and always would be. He had tried to make that clear a couple of times to reporters who asked him how it felt to be a layman again. He had given up his clerical state voluntarily he tried to explain, which meant he no longer functioned as a priest. But the Sacrament of Holy Orders had changed him spiritually, as it did all men when they became priests. There was no such thing as going back.

The distinction didn't seem to mean much to them, but it did to him, if only because it preserved some connection to the only way of life he known for years. He was grateful for that connection the day he received his Rescript of Laicization from the Vatican, basically a document which tells a priest who is leaving the Church what he can and can't do.

For instance, a laicized priest is not supposed to live where his status as an ex-priest is known. But Fitz found difficulty with that right off the bat because he was known all over. It was hard to imagine where he could have gone in order to satisfy that requirement. In the end, he received his Bishop's permission to remain living in New York.

But the Rescript isn't only about restrictions. It also outlines a laicized priest's rights, including his right – his duty, in fact – to hear deathbed confessions when asked. It was a right he had been called on to exercise only a month earlier, when he was awakened by a phone call asking him to rush to Roosevelt Hospital.

Fr. Romero had suffered a heart attack and wasn't expected to pull through, he was told. There were other priests with him at the hospital, but he insisted on seeing his old friend. Fitz raced uptown and got there in time to hear his confession, and even sat up with him until he died less than an hour later. It was the most bittersweet experience of Fitz's life.

He had no regrets about leaving, except for the difficulty it had caused the Church, which was unavoidable. Such a thing is always hard for the Church as well as for the priest, but when the priest is as high-profile as Fitz it's bound to attract a lot of attention, which it did for a while.

But the dust did settle eventually, for a short while at least, until he announced his intention to write a book about the experiences which led to his departure. That kicked it up again. And so, almost two years to the day since Mary first came to him, his story was news again.

It was mid-afternoon, and he was waiting at La Guardia airport with Becca to board a flight to Los Angeles, where she would be covering the press conference that officially launched the book, entitled *Three Days with Mary*. It was already a guaranteed best-seller and the big, good-looking author and ex-priest who knew more than a little about making public appearances was doing everything his publicist could have hoped for and more to promote it.

"You know, Fitz," Becca began again, "we should be heading to our gate already."

He looked at his watch. "I know. Just a few more minutes. I'm sure she'll be here."

Not sure maybe, but he certainly did hope. Interestingly enough, the Rescript of Laicization does not release a priest from all of his vows – it does not release him from his vow of celibacy. An ex-priest can not get married in the Church without first being granted what is called a dispensation from the obligation of celibacy. He can only get that from the Pope, and it is not something which is granted easily or quickly.

Some ex-priests wait many years for a dispensation. Fitz had been waiting a little over eighteen months. He hoped that because the spotlight was on him the Church might move a little more quickly in his case in order to avoid appearing harsh or vindictive. He hoped that for over eighteen months, right up until two weeks earlier when a friend called from Rome to say that he should expect good news sooner rather than later. Since then Fitz had hardly been able to do anything but wait and watch the mail.

As their flight was announced over the loudspeaker a

moment later, Becca looked up to see Marianne walking quickly towards them from the other side of the terminal, right on cue. She was holding a letter up high over her head, waving it excitedly.

Becca closed her laptop and put it in her bag and stood up. She smiled at Fitz and said, "You guys will want a few minutes to talk," and walked off.

END

OCD In
The Serengeti

Some of the best days of Shane's life took place in recording studios. Some of the worst too, something which he didn't find at all surprising since the process of making records was not an easy one, as anyone who had ever taken part in it could attest.

The atmosphere could be stressful because the outcome was never anything but uncertain, with songs constantly being revised, completely rewritten, or in some cases even abandoned right up until the very end. Even to someone with his considerable experience, the goings-on in a studio often seemed more arbitrary than workmanlike. Songs tended to come together by fits and starts, not with the predictability of cars rolling off an assembly line.

Few people really understood this in Shane's experience. Most seemed to think that each new record was manufactured more than created, the result of proper planning as much as inspiration.

The misconception was understandable in his view since what most people knew, or thought they knew about recording was based on what they had seen of it in movies or on television, where more often than not it was portrayed as a fairly neat, efficient, and even happy process. People tended to smile a lot while making records in movies, he noticed.

Of course, there were smiles in real life, too. Some days he smiled a great deal while he worked. Other days, not so much. Balance was the thing, he had heard himself say often. That was what he went for. A single day spent turning lead into gold, transforming a simple tune he had dreamt up into a song he was proud of could make him forget all the frustrating days that preceded it, days when all he got for his efforts was more lead.

He had learned long ago that bad days were not just something to be endured, they were actually an essential part of the creative process. You couldn't make a decent record without suffering through days when nothing sounded right any more than you could get through a winning football game without getting hit. No pain, no gain.

Acceptable bad days aside, Shane only ever had one truly unhappy recording experience. Not surprisingly, it was his very first record, which he made back in 1970 when he was just twenty years old.

Obvious reasons were to blame for the difficulty. For instance, he and his band, The Sharps landed their first recording deal on the strength of their reputation as a great live band. But they had absolutely no studio experience and when recording began they found the whole process alien and decidedly uninspiring.

Also, like most first records the venture was rushed and underfunded, which meant the band had to record from midnight to eight each morning at a substandard studio. And of course the small label they were recording for, Big Apple Records, was anxious to protect its investment in their untested new act, and so got far too involved in everything they did.

Big Apple could almost be forgiven for their initial over-protectiveness. Whereas they were an American company based in New York, The Sharps were Irish. No one in the band had ever set foot in America until then. They were signed sight unseen, on the recommendation of an A&R man who saw them perform in London.

The Big Apple executive responsible for bringing the band across the Atlantic to make their debut record, Billy Mitchell knew little if anything about Ireland, and even less about the band before they met for the first time in the crowded arrivals terminal at Kennedy airport. It took Billy years to admit it to anyone, but he was surprised and relieved that first day to find that Irishmen spoke English.

Although Shane would go on to adopt New York wholeheartedly – in fact, it had been his home ever since then - he was little more than an energetic kid far from home back in 1970. He still considered it a small miracle that their first record ever got made, and a not-so-small miracle that it sold as well as it did – it went gold within a year. More than that, it launched a fairly successful career for The Sharps that saw four more albums released and certified gold before they broke up seven years later.

His own solo career, which began right after that in 1977 owed everything to that first record, as well. It was on the back of that record, and on the record's first single, Approaching Dawn, that his entire reputation as a first rate blues guitarist and singer was built.

For that reason, although he had no real love for that first record, the gold disc he received for it occupied a prominent place on the wall of his studio. It hung right inside the door and was the first thing any visitor saw upon entering. There were a good many other gold records beside it, but that one was first.

Shane thought about giving his studio a name when he first built it a few years before – The Shane Christian Studio was an obvious choice, but it was only one of the names in

the running. Inshane was another, as was Approaching
Dawn. He went so far as to have a designer play with logos
for the front door, but in the end he gave it no official name
once he decided that he was never going to rent it out or try
to make any sort of business out of it. It would be used when
he was using it, otherwise it would be empty. For that
reason, it was just referred to as, "My studio," when he
talked about it or, "Shane's studio," when someone else did.

Occasionally someone referred to it as his home studio.
Although he never bothered to say so, he didn't really
understand that term. Yes, the studio was attached to his
home, but it was so far removed from it in atmosphere and
function that it may as well have been built on the moon.

He felt anything but "at home" when he was in there, and
it wasn't just the obvious things that were responsible for
that, such as the dozens of microphone stands that populated
the main room, the car-sized mixing board, or the drum kit
that lurked in the corner behind the glass. It was everything -
every metal surface, every piece of soundproofing or
blinking light, every windowless wall set the place apart
from his home.

There was something else too, and he was sure that he
could have explained it if he wanted to, but he was never
really sure how it would sound. None of it made him feel
relaxed or comfortable, he would have said. That's what
home is for. Comfort is what he expected from the sofa in
his living room, or the extra-wide door on his refrigerator.
But the studio made him feel edgy and anxious. It raised in
him feelings that could only be stilled by working, by
devoting hour after hour to creating something of value. To
him, that place was a challenge and an encouraging shove
forward all rolled into one, and as far as he was concerned
that was exactly how it should be.

It was in that studio that he had just finished recording his latest CD, his first in five years. He had decided to hold his first major interview in almost that long right there where all the work had been done. Rather than step out of that familiar atmosphere, he wanted his interviewer to step into it.

He was sure that he could guess many of the questions that would be put to him by the average reporter even before they were asked - some of them would be obvious, after all. But the reporter that was coming was not average. She was talented and original. She was bound to ask questions that others wouldn't. It was inevitable. As his ex-wife, she knew him better than most. No doubt, on some days, she still felt she knew him better than he knew himself, something she must have told him a thousand times.

He looked up at the wall clock. Five minutes to two. She was due at two, so she would be there in five minutes. Exactly. The girl was as punctual as a moon shot.

As he often did when preparing for someone or something, he boiled whatever was happening down to the bare facts in order to feel on top of it. Remove the drama and the guesswork, keep only the outline and the dates. So:

1) He met Guinevere Ward in 1994, when she interviewed him for the small music paper she was working for.

2) They began dating immediately afterwards and they were married the following year, when he was 45 and she was 25. It was the first and only marriage for both of them.

3) They divorced amicably five years later.

That was it. Their year of dating, five years of marriage, and subsequent thirteen years of friendship was brought down to just that for the time being.

Shane looked up again at the clock and smiled when his assistant, Johnny poke his head into the room and said, "Guinevere's car just pulled into the driveway." Two o'clock, exactly.

"Okay, just show her in. Thanks."

"Them."

"What?"

"Them. There's someone with her. She's not alone."

That surprised him. Guinevere had said nothing to him about bringing anyone, and she was not usually one for surprises.

"She's not? Are you sure?"

"Yeah. There's two of them in the car."

"Really? Who'd she bring?"

Johnny shrugged. "Don't know. I only caught a glimpse of her through the car window. No one I recognized."

"Her? A woman?"

"Yeah."

"Older? Younger?"

"Younger, probably around twenty-five. Maybe her assistant, or something."

"Hm. Okay."

He might not have realized until that moment how much he had been looking forward to a little one-on-one time with her, but the unexpected addition of another person did nothing to change his mood. He was still looking forward to seeing her.

They rarely got together anymore, despite the fact that geographically they were very close. In fact, the drive from his house to hers would have taken no more than thirty minutes. But what separated them was not so much the miles, but the fact that they were two very different people. He always thought that was almost too neatly reflected in the fact that they inhabited completely different worlds, regardless of how close they were.

Guinevere lived on the top floor of a townhouse in

Hoboken, just across the river from where she worked in mid-town Manhattan. His house was also close to Manhattan, barely thirty minutes north of the city in Chappaqua – not a town, he was constantly reminded by his neighbors when he called it that, but a hamlet within the town of Newcastle.

He had no idea exactly what a hamlet was (versus, say a town or a village) or why his home resided in a place-within-a-place, but as an Irishman he understood instinctively that with land came all kinds of divisions and boundaries, especially the kind you didn't quite get. And he understood one other thing - whatever the particulars, if it was your land you had the right to be proud of it. And he was. A number of buildings near his house, that is to say buildings in the hamlet of Chappaqua within the town of New Castle, were listed in the National Register of Historic Places. He liked that and always got that part right.

He also knew a little something about where Guinevere lived in Hoboken, which he never referred to as a hamlet or a town, but a city, which it was. Despite that, he thought of it as less a part of New Jersey than an unofficial extra borough of New York since so many of its residents were de facto New Yorkers, commuting to Manhattan each and every day by the boatload, trainload, or busload, just as Guinevere did.

Of course, Hoboken was not without a history of its own. The first recorded baseball game was played there in 1846 at a place called Elysian Fields. Frank Sinatra was also born there. But Hoboken had undergone a major facelift from the 1970's through the 1990's that saw a lot of its history plowed under to make room for new condos to house all the commuters. Even the actual site of that fateful ballgame was lost forever under the newly-poured foundations. In that sense, it was a very new place.

However close Hoboken and Chappaqua might appear to be on a map, they lived worlds apart. He knew he could never be comfortable in her world, and she could never sit still for very long in his. But then, that was old news. They had come to that realization thirteen years before.

"Hi!" she said as she walked in, followed first by her friend, and then by Johnny. Then, "Oh, you grew your beard back. Well, a gray one where the brown one used to be, anyway."

He ran his hand over his chin and smiled. "Yeah, I missed it."

"Well, it looks nice. Just tell me you won't grow the hair again." Around the studio there were photographs of Shane at different stages of his career. Some showed him with a beard, others showed him clean-shaven, but in all the photos from the first half of his career he had shoulder-length hair. Anything from the last fifteen years showed him with the close-cropped haircut he was still wearing then.

"Don't worry. I wouldn't have the patience."

He was standing by then, and they met in a warm hug in the middle of the large room before she introduced the other woman. "Shane, this is Cleo. Cleo, Shane Christian."

He shook Cleo's hand and said, "It's nice to meet you."

"Cleo is working with us as, doing an internship. She's studying to be a journalist, and I thought this would be great experience for her, hanging out with a bona fide rock star. Is that okay?"

"Of course it is." And then to Cleo, "You're very welcome, Cleo."

"It's a real pleasure to meet you. I really love your work."

"Thank you, that's very nice of you to say."

He motioned for them to sit down, but then shook his head when he realized there weren't enough chairs. There were only the two he had arranged for himself and Guinevere.

"Oh, Johnny, would you mind pulling another chair over?" he asked.

Johnny wheeled the third chair from across the room, putting it right beside one of the others, but Shane quickly repositioned all three so they were in a triangle. He didn't want to feel like he was being ganged up on.

Guinevere dropped her bag on the floor beside one of the chairs and sat down, followed by Cleo.

Johnny asked, "Can I get either of you something to drink?"

Guinevere just smiled and shook her head. Cleo said, "I'm fine, thank you." Johnny then looked to Shane, who lifted the bottle of water he was already holding and said, "I'm good. Thanks."

"Okay," said Johnny. "I'll be around. Just call if you need anything."

"Will do."

With that Johnny left, closing the door behind him.

"So, how have you been?" Guinevere asked as Shane took his seat. It was a reasonable first question.

"Good. I've been good. You?"

"Oh, I have no complaints," she said.

"I'm glad to hear it."

Guinevere paused for just a moment, then smiled and said, "Before we get started can I ask you something?"

"Shoot."

"Why me?"

"Why you, what?"

"Why do I get the first interview about your new CD? I mean, I'm very grateful, you know that, but I wondered why."

He supposed that was a reasonable second question, as

well.

"You mean aside from the fact that you're a respected journalist and you know I've always said you have great taste in music?"

"Yeah, aside from that."

"Well, I'm afraid that's it, really. Why, does there have to be some other reason?"

"No, there doesn't have to be. Not necessarily. But…"

"But what?"

"There could be."

It was his turn to smile. "Like what? What would my other reason be?"

"My insight."

"I'm sorry? Your insight into what?"

"Into you, of course. Maybe you figure I'll understand your new work better than just another journalist - say, someone who was never married to you. I mean, anyone could appreciate it, but maybe you wanted someone who could really understand it."

"I'm not following you. Understand what, exactly?"

"Well, this CD, coming at this stage in your career, at this stage in your life… a lot of folks expect there to be a heavy emphasis on, let's say time. You know, where you've been, and where you find yourself now."

"Oh. An introspective piece? An exploration of my own life and times?"

"If you like. What's gone right over the years, what's gone wrong, where it's brought you… that sort of thing. And if that's the case, maybe you feel that our shared history will give me some insight into that, since I know a bit more about you than most."

He shook his head. "I see. Well no, it's nothing like that, believe me. This CD is not about where I find myself now, to borrow your phrase, or anything that would require your special insight."

That didn't seem to convince her, so she continued.

"People always speculate as to the reason whenever an artist makes them wait for new material. You know how it goes, you know this business better than I do. And in your case, well, your fans have been waiting a long time.

"A colleague of mine suggested that when artists of a certain age take a long time - five years, in your case - to make a record it's because something has made them look inward. The result is introspective songs. Songs about regret, or past mistakes, what have you."

She paused before adding, "I'll be honest with you. He even suggested that I might be in there – a little or a lot." She delivered that last line with the kind of smile a child uses when they ask for permission to open a Christmas gift early.

He laughed and shook his head again. "I'm sorry to disappoint you, but it's nothing like that. It's not a middle-aged man record in any way."

She gave a wicked smirk. "I'm middle-aged, my Dear. You are the thing that comes next."

Cleo tried to stifle her laugh but a bit of it escaped, followed by a guilty look. Shane knew better than to argue a point he couldn't win, so he simply threw up his hands. "Okay then, it's not an old man's record, either. Really, there's nothing about it that has anything to do with this or any stage in life."

After saying that he looked at her for a moment, then added, "That's ironic."

"What is?"

"What you just suggested. Funny enough, I was trying to do almost the exact opposite thing on this CD. I purposely avoided writing a 'summing-up' record by keeping myself more or less out of it. Out of the lyrics, I mean."

"How could you avoid injecting yourself into your own songs?"

"Well, I couldn't. Not completely, anyway. But rather than give it all away I tried to be a bit vague as I wrote these songs. Whatever I might have had in mind, whatever started me writing a song in the first place, I would only hint at it or dance around it, maybe even adopt a different point of view, just so long as I didn't reveal too much.

"That sounds like I was trying to be coy, I know, but I wasn't. It's just that 'exploration' wasn't my reason for making the CD, so I figured if I didn't lay too much out there, there was less chance that people would try to read between the lines, and end up misinterpreting everything."

She nodded for a long while as she took in what he said and eventually accepted it. Finally, she asked, "So, what's it called?"

"Ah." He raised a finger, then reached behind his chair and pulled out a manila envelope which he handed to her. She pulled out the single sheet from inside and examined the artwork for the CD cover, leaning over so that Cleo could also see it. After a moment she said, "*OCD In the Serengeti*? That's the title?"

"Mm, hm."

"I like that," said Cleo, speaking for the first time. "That title conjures up a lot of images."

"And no specific one, I hope. Again, that was the point of the title, of the songs... I really wanted, in essence, for the glass to be a bit frosted so it wasn't so easy to see through."

Guinevere examined it some more. The cover featured a striking picture of a wildebeest migration – countless thousands of them as far as the eye could see. In the foreground was a man with his back to the camera, watching them, visible only as a dark silhouette because of the darkening sky. His identity was further obscured by the way the picture was cropped – the man was cut off above the neck and below the knees. After staring at it for a minute or two, she looked up.

"This is you. In the photograph." She pointed to the paper. "It's you."

"How do you know it's…"

"Those are your hands. I can tell."

He tried not to smile at that. At least, outwardly. To himself he smiled at the thought of an old lover recognizing his hands in a photograph, knowing what made them different from anyone else's. To him there was an implied connection in that, a sort of intimacy. It was enough to make their years together even more profound in his mind – what they had may not have lasted, but it hadn't vanished completely if at least the ghost of it still hovered in how well she knew him.

"When were you in Africa?" she asked.

"About a year ago."

She nodded her head again. "Nice, very nice. So, is the title in any way…"

"Relevant? No. In fact there's no song called 'OCD In the Serengeti' on the CD. There's no song on it that relates to the cover in any way."

"*OCD In the Serengeti,*" she said again under her breath. She turned to Cleo. "It has an interesting ring to it, doesn't it?"

Cleo nodded. "Yes, it hints at opposites in a way - East meets West, or old versus new."

"Mm, hm. I like that Shane, I really do. So, tell me about these songs that apparently won't be about whatever they might sound like they're supposed to be about."

He smiled and made a revolving motion with his finger. "Oh," she said, and turned the paper over to find the artwork for the back cover. In stark contrast to the front, there were no wildebeests, no hands, no design of any kind, really – just the credits and song titles in simple white letters on a black background.

Guinevere began reading silently. After a moment she looked up and pointed to the page. "Is this a typo?"

"Where?"

"Here. The second song… 'The Bread of Comminion'. Is that right, Comminion?"

"Yes, that's it."

After a moment she asked, "Is that a word?" He only smiled and shrugged.

"I see," she said, and continued reading down the list, this time out loud. "'Sister Wing and Yoko,' 'The Bread of Comminion,' 'Blues in A minus,' 'Landlocked Wharf Rat,'…"

She lowered the page and looked up. "These are some pretty interesting titles. Want to tell me about some of them?"

"Sure. The idea was…"

"Wait, wait, hold on. I didn't know you went to Africa."

He found that a strange remark, coming from his ex-wife. He was about to ask why on earth she would know that, or why she would know about much of anything he was up to for that matter, but he couldn't think of a way to keep it from sounding like a challenge. So, instead he settled for, "Yes, I did."

"How was it?"

"It was great. Beyond great. Really, a fantastic trip."

She kept her eyes on him and tilted her head. "We used to travel a great deal. Together. We travelled a lot."

"Um, yes. We did."

"We went around the world a few times as I recall, but we never went to Africa."

He thought for a moment, then said, "That's true." But that answer didn't seem to do it for her. She kept staring at him accusingly, so he continued. "We never went to the North Pole, either. We mostly travelled for work, didn't we? On tours, and such. I didn't play too many shows in Africa. Or the North Pole."

"You used to go along on tours?" Cleo interjected, wide-eyed.

Guinevere heard the fascination in her voice and fixed her with a big smile. "Most of the time. And if you're thinking, 'Wow you're so lucky!' you're right. It was a hell of an experience, and a lot of fun."

Turning back to Shane, she said, "Still, I don't recall you ever expressing any desire to go on safari or anything like that, even for a vacation."

"No? Well, you're probably right. It was kind of a spur-of-the-moment thing."

She looked at him hard for a moment. "I don't recall you ever being a spur-of-the-moment kind of guy, either."

He put up his hands in a hopeless gesture. "People change. It's been known to happen."

"Not you. You were more this type..." She held up the paper and pointed to the OCD in the CD title. She turned towards Cleo and pointed again. For no particular reason that she knew of, Cleo nodded as if agreeing.

He laughed and rolled his head back. "That again? Really? No matter how many times you claim I had, or have OCD it isn't true."

Guinevere only raised her eyebrows.

He leaned towards Cleo. "No matter what she says, I don't

have OCD. I was never diagnosed with it, have never suffered from it, right?" he said. Cleo, having no clue what she suddenly seemed to find herself in the middle of simply nodded again.

He continued in a patient voice – it was obvious that he and Guinevere had been down that road before. "The fact is I grew up in a very small house in Galway. There were eight of us, all underfoot. There was hardly any room as it was, and if we weren't neat it would have been completely unlivable. That's just how I was raised." He poked a thumb in Guinevere's direction. "I've told her that a thousand times."

"Yeah, you've told me," Guinevere answered in a mock-sarcastic voice.

Shane continued to Cleo, "She just always hated that I was much neater than her. And that wasn't..." He left off there, but just a little too late. Guinevere leaned forward and punched his arm.

"Go on, say it. Say it. ...and that wasn't hard because she was such a slob."

"I wasn't going to say that. I was going to say... Well like I said, people change. I'm sure you're much... you know, not a slob now."

She shook her head. "No. No, I still throw everything everywhere. The only difference is no one picks up after me now. What about you?"

"What about me?"

"Do you still, you know... do all those things? Like, the shoelaces?" She asked the question with a smile that was meant to ward off his exasperation, but which didn't really work.

"Oh, my God. Do you mean, am I still a neat person? Yes, I am. And that is not the same thing as having OCD, by the way. The shoelaces… that's not a compulsive thing, either. That's just keeping my hands clean."

Cleo raised a hand high in the air slowly, like a school girl who was afraid to admit she had fallen behind. "I'm sorry. Can I just ask… what's 'the shoelaces'?

"Oh, my God," he said again. "It's absolutely nothing, believe me. Nothing we have to go into."

Guinevere let out a big laugh at that, and said, "Oh, come on, now. Tell her. Let her make up her own mind." When Cleo turned an expectant look his way he knew he was cornered. He could only shake his head and try – but fail - to keep the smile from his face.

After a moment he drew up straight and said, "Okay. What she's referring to is my habit of tucking my shoelaces into my shoes when I take them off so the laces won't get dirty. As I've told your colleague here repeatedly, if the laces are loose and they wind up under your shoes they pick up everything you walked on all day. Then you get that on your hands the next time you tie your shoes."

Cleo pursed her lips, happy to have some idea what she was agreeing or disagreeing with. "Makes sense," she said.

"Thank you."

Shane shrugged at Guinevere, but she only laughed harder. "Do you have any idea how that sounds?"

"Well, it wouldn't sound like anything if you didn't make me say it."

"Uh, huh. Nice rationale." After a moment she said, "How about the other things. The cookies? The Oreos?" That only got a sigh from him. "Do you still have to eat them two at a time?" she continued.

"I don't have to. I never had to. I prefer to. Oreos are fucking awesome. One isn't enough."

"One isn't enough? Well, what about three? Or five? You

always had to break one in half if I ever mistakenly gave you an odd number, making it even."

He sat still, just smiling to himself and waiting for her to finish. She knew what she knew, or thought she knew - there was no getting around that.

"Yes. I like eating in two's," he said finally. "I like things even. Look, I'm a songwriter. Almost everything I do - the rhythms I use, the lines of lyrics I create – most of it is built in two's, four's, what have you. It's just the way I think."

"That's true, Shane. Come to think of it, you always liked doing everything in two's," she said with a sexy wink.

With that they both burst into laughter. Cleo joined in a moment later with a wide-eyed look that betrayed her thoughts - she was getting far more out of the trip than she ever could have imagined on the ride out there.

Shane was happy to let the exchange end in laughter. He couldn't recall how many similar debates they had stumbled into during their marriage, but there were many because Guinevere's description of them was accurate - he was a very neat, orderly person and she was not.

She loved teasing him about that and she threw around the term OCD very easily back then, sometimes jokingly, sometimes not. Often, he would try to school her in the difference between a preference and a compulsion. Now, he was happy just to laugh it off.

The fact was, his new CD had been named for that very thing, but only as an inside joke which luckily, Guinevere didn't seem to fully get. She was right of course, the man in the picture was him. Anyone might have guessed that seeing as it was his CD, but few would have known it for sure, as she did.

She rightly identified him by his hands, but thankfully she seemed not to notice what those hands were doing. They were counting. His whole purpose in going to Africa was to relax and get away from everything familiar for a while, but in a lifetime of heavy travel he had found many times that his love of order accompanied him everywhere he went, even across the ocean. Even to a plain where he found himself face-to-face with a million disorderly wildebeests.

He wasn't actually trying to count them, of course. He didn't have quite the obsession with numbers or pairs that one might think he did listening to Guinevere. But he would be the last to deny that he had little quirks, played little number games which could make it seem that way.

What he was trying to do at the moment the picture was taken was focus on a single spot in the distance and count how many animals passed it in a minute's time. It was completely impossible, of course. He gave up in seconds. But funny enough, it was during those very seconds that the photographer captured that cover image. She caught him red-handed, literally. What Guinevere seemed to have missed when she recognized his hands – thankfully - was that one or two fingers were extended on either one, counting.

It was intended to be a very inside joke – between him and him. He was glad that it still was.

"Okay, back to the songs," Guinevere said. "Any personal favorites?"

"Hm. I quite like 'What size shirt does Julio wear?'" And 'Damn'. I like 'Damn' very much."

She looked again at the track listing. "'Damn.' The last song?"

"Mm, hm."

"Do you want to tell me what 'Damn' is about?"

Shane started to answer, then stood up. "I've got a better idea. Why don't I play if for you? Then you can tell me what you think it's about." He looked from one to the other as they nodded enthusiastically.

"Great. Give me just a moment."

As he turned and walked to the control room, Cleo leaned towards Guinevere. She couldn't help smiling as she hissed in an exited whisper, "This hasn't even been released yet. This is awesome!"

Guinevere loved what a great time Cleo was having, and she was glad to be giving her such an exciting introduction to the business. With a smile she answered, "More than that... this probably hasn't even been heard by anyone outside of this studio yet – DJs, the record company... nobody." Then she added, "You're one of the first to ever hear it." Cleo sat back in her chair, beaming.

As the music started playing, loud and crystal clear through the studio monitors, Guinevere smiled to Shane, who had returned from the control room and was standing with his hands on the back of his chair.

Her smile conveyed a lot – she was pleased by what she heard. She loved the overall sound. She loved the sound of his guitar in particular and his playing style, which she always said she could recognize anywhere. When he began singing she loved the sound of his voice, which sounded just like it always had. Shane never had the strongest of voices, but it was always passionate and believable, and the passion was still there as she listened to him sing the first chorus of 'Damn'.

You've got the wrong man,
I don't give a damn about you.
Let your whores pretend to do that
for the money you pay them.

Her smile only broadened as he sang the next lines, his

voice growing more thick and gritty to match the venom in his lyrics.

I'm like your Mommy and Daddy
who must have dreamed of ditching you,
turning you away for nothing but
the trouble it would save them.

When the song was over Shane stopped the CD and returned to his seat. "So?"

Guinevere said quietly, "That's terrific, Shane."

Cleo was not nearly as quiet. "That was fantastic! Really, really great!"

"Thank you. So!" He smiled and held his hands out to both of them. "What's it about?"

Guinevere was the first to answer. "Well, it's about a bank robbery, of course. A hold-up. But, it doesn't go the way the robbers expect it to."

"No, it doesn't."

"When they pull out their guns they expect everyone in the bank to be afraid and do what they're told, but one guy refuses. One of the employees."

Shane nodded. "A teller."

"Right. This one teller won't hand over the money, won't cooperate at all. He just stands there damning the thief who's pointing a gun at him."

"He's dying," Cleo added, "The teller is dying, so he doesn't feel like he's got anything to lose."

He nodded his head. "Yeah, that's it. It starts off like a big story because there are a lot of people in the bank – customers, employees, robbers - but it quickly comes down to just those two.

"The first man, the robber is willing to risk his own life,

even take someone else's life in order to get what he wants. He goes in there feeling pretty powerful. The other guy, the teller is feeling completely powerless. He has very little time left and he can't do anything about it – can't change it, can't stop it.

"But he realizes as soon as his life is threatened that it's meaningless - no one can take away from him something which he hasn't got. He realizes he's not so powerless after all because he can still say no. He can say or do anything he wants without fear of the consequences.

"The robber was not unprepared for a challenge, but he thought it would come from a guard or the police. Instead he finds an ordinary man standing between him and what he wants not because he cares so much, but because he doesn't care at all."

Guinevere tilted her head. "That's very interesting. Of course, you didn't go into quite that much detail in the song."

"No. That's what I was getting at before... being a bit vague. Let people fill in the blanks, write their own story."

She looked at him for a moment. "So... Are you sick by any chance?"

He smiled. "No, I'm not sick. I'm not going to rob a bank, either. I told you, this CD is not a look inside the soul of a middle-aged... correction, an old man. It's nothing like that. These songs are... stories. Some are based on articles I might have come across, some I pulled out of thin air. They're all personal on some level maybe, in that they mean something to me, but they're fiction. Some of them are, anyway. Almost half of them are instrumentals, actually."

"Really? A highly respected lyric writer is releasing a CD where half the tracks are instrumentals? Any reason?"

"More of the same, really. Looking out, not in. I figure the fewer lyrics I put out there, the less people will feel compelled to dissect and analyze them."

"Got it." She paused, then added, "And you're sure you're not sick?"

He couldn't help but smirk. "I don't even have a cold, trust me."

"Hm," was her only answer. The look that accompanied it said she wasn't sure she did.

He continued. "Also, I feel that I'm playing at a really good level these days, and I wanted the focus to be on that. Sort of like in the early days - the songs were always good, even then, but the records were mostly about the playing, about the sound. I really felt like doing something like that again."

"Can we hear another?" Cleo asked, this time without raising her hand. "What was the other one you mentioned, something about a shirt?"

"'What size shirt does Julio wear?' Sure, hold on." When he got up again to go to the control room, Guinevere asked, "Wanna tell us about this one?"

He turned around, but didn't sit back down. "Oh, sure. It's about distractions, I suppose. And choices... um, no, that's wrong. Not choices. It's about the things that happen to us unexpectedly, the common everyday accidents or surprises, and how they can become important in our lives."

"Like...?"

Cleo jumped forward in her chair. "Like when you walk down the wrong street and bump into someone who turns out to be your soul mate? Like that?" she asked.

"Yes, exactly like that. Although I might have given a different example, like you walk down the wrong street and get killed by falling debris from a construction site."

Guinevere shook her head. "Always so morose. So how

does that idea apply to this song?"

"Well, it's about a guy who's relaxing at home alone on a Saturday when he gets a phone call, someone asking what size shirt Julio wears. The thing is, he doesn't know anyone named Julio, doesn't even know the caller. It's a wrong number.

"But instead of just hanging up he makes a joke about it and the two guys wind up having a friendly little chat for a few minutes. It turns out they don't live far from each other, and he tells the caller of a great store where he can get sports jerseys, which is what he was looking to buy for this guy Julio.

"Anyway, they hang up and that's that... until later that day. The guy is now watching the evening news and what does he see? There was some sort of gas leak and explosion in the town where the jersey store is located. According to the reporter, a whole block was affected. A number of stores were completely destroyed, including that one, the store where he told the caller to go.

"Well, he can't believe it. His mind is full of questions... Did the caller go there? Was he there when the explosion occurred? Had he sent someone to his death accidentally?"

He stopped there, and for a long moment neither woman spoke, unsure if there was more coming. Finally Guinevere said, "Jesus Christ, Shane. Can't you just once write a song about rainbows or pretty flowers or something?"

He didn't even try to keep from smiling. She had asked him similar questions before. Many people had. He was known for dwelling on the darker side of things in his songs. He gave her his stock answer. "There are plenty of songs about rainbows and pretty flowers already."

But Cleo was still waiting to ask the obvious question, "So, did he? The guy on the phone – did he go to the store? I mean, did he die?"

Shane shrugged. "You know, I really can't say. I could never quite decide how I wanted that to go. In the end I left the question open. In the song, I mean. What happens is… Well, I'll tell you what. I'll play it for you. You tell me what you think of how it ends up, okay?"

Cleo nodded her head quickly.

This time Shane didn't come back into the room when the music started playing. He remained in the control booth, watching their reactions through the large window.

Again, he could see Guinevere taking it all in the way she always did – deciphering each new guitar lick and drum roll, listening as critically to the mix and the arrangement as she did to the lyrics, and smiling to herself whenever something really worked. She sat back with her eyes closed until the song was over, hardly moving, not missing a beat.

Cleo, on the other hand, sat on the edge of her chair staring at the floor by her feet. Her elbows were resting on her knees, and she held her chin in her hands. She was working the whole time, searching for bits of information. She was trying to listen through the music. To her the notes were like windows – they might be pretty, but what really interested her was what was going on behind them.

He could see her nod her head almost imperceptibly at the end of each verse, digesting more and more of the story. The look of concentration never left her face once. The more she heard, the more she invested herself in the characters, and the more she wanted to know how their stories ended.

When the last verse began, Shane could see Guinevere's appreciation for the overdubbed guitars that kicked in, punctuating each line about the fire and its aftermath. In Cleo's face he could see the intensity of someone racing towards the last page of a crime novel, desperate to find out how it ends. Her eyebrows raised as he sang the final lines.

Three days, and I'm still looking at your number,
but nothing more than that.
If I dialed and you answered,
If I dialed and you didn't,
If I dialed and you couldn't,
What would I say, what would I ask?
What could I call myself at last?

"So, he never finds out if the guy died?" Cleo asked Shane as soon as he came back into the room.

"Nope," Shane said, almost apologetically. "He still had the guy's number on his phone, but even after some days he couldn't bring himself to call and find out. Or, wouldn't."

As Cleo was thinking about that, Johnny walked into the studio. He pointed to the control room. "Sorry, I just need to get something."

"No sweat." Shane answered.

Johnny took only a moment to do what he had to do in the control room, then turned and headed back out of the studio. As he passed them he said, "I heard you playing 'What size shirt does Julio wear?' I love that song."

"Thanks."

As he opened the door to leave, Johnny called over his shoulder, "It's too bad the guy had to die."

Cleo's head whipped around. "What?! Hey! Why did you say that?"

Johnny poked his head back into the room a bit sheepishly. "Me?"

"Yeah. Why did you say he died?" Cleo demanded.

He shrugged. "I don't know. That was just the impression I got."

"Why?"

Without moving from his position, half-hidden behind the door, he said, "Well, I figure that if I was in his shoes, the guy who called that is, and someone had sent me to a place which subsequently blew up – yet, I survived – I would find that significant. And knowing that the guy who sent me there might be feeling responsible, I'd call just to say I was okay. I would want to let him off the hook, in case he was worried. But he didn't do that, so I figured, you know... he was dead." After a moment, he added, "Okay?"

"Well, maybe the guy had already deleted the number from his phone," Cleo said. "Maybe he lost his phone. Maybe he just wasn't that polite and it just didn't occur to him to call."

After a moment, Johnny repeated, "Okay."

"He could still be alive."

And once more. "Okay."

Shane decided it was time to help Johnny escape. "Thanks, Johnny." With that, Johnny nodded and let the door close behind him.

With an amused smile, Guinevere said, "Perhaps we can hear one of the instrumentals."

"Sure. How about 'Landlocked Wharf Rat'? I like that one."

"Anything to the title?"

"Mmmm, not really, no. I've just always liked that phrase, wharf rat. I thought it would be funny to turn it around, you know? Take a character that survives by the water and cut him off from it... like a driver with no car, or a bird with no wings, that sort of thing.

"The music has... well, you'll hear, it has a halting feeling to it. It keeps stopping and starting, changing tempos and keys. I thought the title should sound as unsettled as the tune.

"Wait, I'll put it on for you."

"Landlocked Wharf Rat" was the longest of the songs he had played so far, almost eight minutes. After starting it he returned to his seat to enjoy it with them. He was very proud of the tune, which was actually a collection of tunes he had written over a long period of time. He had worked long and hard to combine them into a single piece that was cohesive, with a couple of identifiable themes running throughout, despite the constantly shifting time signatures and keys.

As the tune played he could see Guinevere, her eyes closed again, tilting her head this way and that as the various changes occurred.

Shane leaned in her direction. "Order from chaos," he whispered. She smiled knowingly, but didn't open her eyes.

Shane saw Cleo watching the exchange. He leaned closer to her. "That was something I always used to tell her about my songwriting process. When I was trying to create a piece that was more or less complicated, it was like creating order from chaos. That's how it felt to me, like I was pulling the pieces together, taming them."

Cleo smiled, grateful to be clued in.

When the song was over, Shane went once more to the control room to turn the CD off.

"So," he said when he sat down again, "That's a taste of what this CD is all about."

"It's wonderful, Shane," Guinevere said. "It's going to be a pleasure writing about this stuff. It's not a re-hash of old material, not a CD of covers that inspired you when you were fifteen, not a weak attempt to bring the past to life or to follow some new trend... None of that obvious bullshit. Just a great new CD from someone at the top of his game. Period."

"Thank you. I'm so glad that you see it that way. That's

exactly what I was going for. I want to leave the music writers nothing to say except they like it, or they don't. I'll be fine with either one, as long as they don't try to examine me looking for a story that isn't there."

Guinevere looked at him for a long moment, then said, "Well, on that note..." She gathered up her purse and got up to go, and Cleo followed suit.

Guinevere and Shane exchanged another warm hug, and then Shane shook Cleo's outstretched hand.

"I still say he survived," she said with a smile before letting go. Shane could only smirk and add, "As you said, he could have lost the number. It happens all the time." That got one final enthusiastic nod.

With that, Shane walked them to the studio door. As they were about to pass through, Guinevere turned to Cleo and said, "You go ahead. I'll be right there."

"Okay, sure." Cleo looked at Shane. "Thank you again, it was a real pleasure. I think the CD is fantastic."

"Thank you. Thank you very much."

Guinevere teasingly said to her, "And if you see poor Johnny on the way out, please don't attack him."

Cleo smiled at that and left. When the door closed behind her, Guinevere turned to Shane. "You know what I'm going to ask you."

Shane put on a mock-worried face. "Wait, I don't owe you any alimony, do I?"

That got him another solid punch in the arm. "I'm serious."

"Ow! No, I don't know what you're going to ask me. What?"

She let out an exasperated breath. "Are you? Sick, I mean?"

He placed his hand over his heart. "I swear to you, I am

not sick."

"And the reason for all this? All your adult life you've been laying your thoughts out there for everyone to pick over, and now suddenly you don't want to?"

Shane smiled at that. "I ask you, isn't that reason enough?"

She looked at him, judging his answer.

"I just felt like playing for a change," he continued, "playing and singing. Not confessing. That's all."

She continued looking at him a short while longer.

"And you're not sick?"

With a weary smile, he shook his head. "No. Thank you. Really, I thank you, but no."

After a moment she gave a quick nod and with that, she seemed to accept his answer, finally. She stood up tall and said, "Well, you look great. And your playing is terrific, Shane. Really. As good as ever."

"Thank you."

As she turned to go, she said, "By the way, don't tell Cleo I said this, but I don't think he lived."

When he looked at her questioningly, she added, "The wrong number guy."

"Oh? Why do you say that?"

"Because the story is nothing without consequences. You can't explore what happens as a result of life's accidents if nothing happens, right? If the end result was always a happy ending, who would care?"

Shane smiled broadly. "That's how I see it too, to be honest. But I think Cleo would disagree with you that happy endings aren't always best."

"She's young, remember what that's like? Let her stumble over a few accidents of her own, a few consequences. She'll see in time – frowns aren't to be feared. They can teach us a lot more than smiles, sometimes."

"Yes, she'll see. Perhaps by the time she's middle-aged... like you."

Guinevere laughed as she turned and started walking away. "Maybe by then she'll be lucky enough to have an old man like you around to teach her these things."

But Shane got the last word and the last laugh. "Only if she's really, really lucky."

END

Truths, Lies, and Contributions

MICHAEL CANAVAN

The truth brings with it
a great measure of absolution, always.
R.D. Laing

Most people attend reunions in an almost schizophrenic state. By the time they pass through the doors of the old gym or the rented banquet hall there's an optimistic part of them that has been gearing itself up for all the great things that it just knows will occur. It's the part that has had them dieting like mad in order to get back down to something like fighting weight, buying new clothes they can't afford, and rehearsing stories of their greatest successes they'll use to make their old friends and enemies gasp.

And then there's the other part, the part that hasn't stopped assuring them since they first received their invitation that no matter what they do to try and avoid it the night will have its share of awkward moments, moments when they wished they had simply stayed home. That part knows that once all the old embarrassing stories are pulled from the closet to be dusted off one by one, they will become exactly who they used to be, or who they were, or who everyone else thought they were a quarter of a century before – the slut, the fat kid, the vandal, whatever. That part knows that not even the sharpest clothes or the most impressive stories will be enough to change them into someone new and different.

But some never have to bother with this dual personality business - those who don't normally suffer from optimism as a rule, for instance. For those lucky few there are no let-downs on such nights. With all their hearts they expect their reunions to be just plain awkward affairs, and so they are.

Mitch was one of those. He expected absolutely nothing good to come of the evening, and so he hadn't gone out of his way to impress anyone before or since arriving. He was quite happy to leave that to everyone else while he just observed and suffered quietly.

That worked pretty well for him for a while. He even managed to enjoy a few of the conversations he got into until one of them suddenly turned on him. Exactly how the hell it did that – and so early in the evening - Mitch didn't know, so at first he wasn't sure exactly who or what to curse. It could have his own fault since he never had to sit at that table in the first place, or even no one's fault. After all, people are expected to talk at reunions, so naturally they have to come up with things to talk about.

Like relationships. Relationships is a natural topic for people getting to know each other again, part of catching up. And so, for a while they talked about a variety of unions, pairings, and marriages among people they knew or used to know. But when the talk suddenly turned to breakups, things began to get awkward for him.

In truth, he wouldn't have minded discussing a breakup, as long as it was someone else's. Someone not at the table, preferably. But not his, for Christ's sake. Not hers. And not with her leading the way. He could hardly believe his own ears when she started talking about it. I mean, just how often does a woman bring up the subject of her own bad breakup when both her husband and her ex-boyfriend are at the table?

Leave it to Liz, he thought. Leave it to her to put him on the spot like that, and leave it to her to do it in the sweetest possible way.

"Well, don't be bashful," she said.

"I'm not being bashful. This just isn't…"

"What? Appropriate? Politically correct?"

"Yes, and yes."

"Come on, it's been five years. You can see I've moved on." Liz gave her husband Tim's hand a loving squeeze as she smiled at him. "Come on," she said again.

"Really, no one wants to hear this." He said those words with all the discomfort in his voice that he could muster, thinking that might get at least one of them to take pity on him, but it didn't work. No one made any move to rescue him.

Instead, they all chimed in right on cue. Of course they wanted to hear it, they all agreed. The mood around the table went from polite camaraderie to every man for himself in a matter of seconds. Someone was in trouble and it wasn't any of them, that was all they cared about.

He really shouldn't have been surprised. Self-preservation aside, they had another reason for going along with her. Although he had gone to high school with almost everyone at the table he had never really known any of them all that well. These were Liz's friends, part of what had been her circle. Naturally, they would have her back before his.

But the deciding moment came when Tim leaned forward and put his two cents in, bringing a big laugh to the whole table in the process.

"Go right ahead, Mitch. Really, maybe I'll learn something about how to deal with my wife in a crisis situation."

Once he said that it was all over. Mitch liked Tim very much, always had. Even in a room full of nice guys, Tim was a nice guy. His reticence to talk about his and Liz's past was based at least in part on not wanting to make her husband uncomfortable, but that excuse was apparently no match for Tim's robust self-esteem.

When he still hesitated, Liz said, "Have you forgotten the question? I asked when you first knew you were going to break up with me." Then she added, "It's not like you ever told me, is it?"

He looked around at all the expectant faces. They all remembered the three short years that he and Liz had called themselves a couple. He was sure that few of them thought fondly of him when they remembered how hurt she was when it ended. Still, he knew that he would look ridiculous if he did anything but start talking, so he took a breath and said, "Okay."

"The truth, now," Liz put in quickly, but she needn't have bothered. He didn't understand why she wanted to do this. He certainly didn't understand why she wanted to do it in this way, in this place. But one thing he did know - if he was going to say anything at all, it was going to be the truth. Even if he could see little point in it, he could see even less point in lying to her.

"There were two things, actually," he began, "two times that I knew I had to go."

"Wow, twice you got on this man's wrong side," said Patricia, one of the sharpest of Liz's sharp friends. He remembered her well from his high school days, by reputation at least. She was known as one of those girls you didn't approach. She had both the looks and the brains to reduce any high school boy to jello if he dared to think he was any kind of match for her. The looks had faded somewhat, but apparently that was all.

"Isn't it supposed to be three strikes, you're out? What did our little angel do wrong, anyway?"

"Nothing," he added quickly. "She did nothing wrong. Both times it was something sweet, actually."

"Tell me," Liz said, then corrected herself as she gestured around the table. "Tell us."

He paused again, but only for a moment. Then he began at a strange place – one of his fondest memories.

"One day... one day I came over to your apartment, the one in Yonkers. I didn't have to knock on the door when I got upstairs. You had left it open for me so I could walk right in. When I did, everything was very still. It was early so all the lights were off, but the stereo was playing really loud. Coldplay. It was the first time I had ever heard them, in fact. It added to the... I don't know, mysterious feeling.

"I didn't see you anywhere, not in the kitchen or the living room. I called into the bedroom but you didn't answer. Then I noticed the balcony door was open. The way the curtains were swaying and everything, it was like an invitation. So, I went out there.

"When I did you were sitting on the floor with your back to the wall. You had a glass of white wine sitting on the floor beside you, and..." He held up his hand and made a little circle with his thumb and his first finger. "And you were smoking a joint."

That got a few laughs from her friends, who knew her recreational habits well.

He continued. "You didn't move a muscle when you saw me. You didn't have to. You were happy just where you were, doing what you were doing. You looked more contented than I had ever seen anyone look in my life. You just smiled up at me and said, 'Hey, lover.'"

Mitch deliberately looked away from Tim as he said that. If there was any sort of reaction, he didn't want to see it.

"I got this feeling. It was like... I don't know how to explain it, really. It was like I had just stepped into another world. The sounds, the sights, the temperature.... everything was different than it had been just minutes before as I sat in my car driving down there. Different than it had been in the parking lot, or even in the elevator.

"And, I knew why. I always knew why because it happened whenever I went there. It was because the moment I stepped into your apartment I was stepping into your life. All the rules were different there, everything was. None of the things I worried about on any other day were supposed to matter on days that I was there, none of the problems of my own life were supposed to follow me through your door.

"I remember just standing there looking at you for a while before I even sat down. You looked so incredibly sweet. The whole moment was sweet. Sweet, and very sexy, and so... hard."

He paused for a moment. "The second time..."

"Wait, wait!" they all objected. How did that qualify as a time he knew he had to break up with her, they all wanted to know.

With a wave of his hand he quieted them down. "Let me finish. They're both the same. The same reason, anyway. You'll see."

After a moment he continued.

"So, the second time was in my apartment, the first one I had after my divorce. You and your daughter - I guess she was about two at the time - came and stayed with me one night. Do you remember? She was really tired when you got there, so you lay down on my bed with her and I lay down beside you and we talked quietly while we waited for her to drift off. But instead we all conked out. We just sort of followed her lead even though it was only about eight o'clock. It was so funny – you drove all that way and all we did was sleep."

"Aw, that's really sweet," said Madeline, another of Liz's friends. "What a picture."

"The thing was, the way you were laying down holding her, you were facing away from me. You didn't turn around – you were afraid to move because you didn't want to wake her up. So, the whole time we were talking you were reaching back with one hand, holding my hand."

"I remember," Liz said. He could tell from her smile that she truly did.

"The way you were laying there - one hand in front holding her and one behind holding me, you were the picture of... I guess completeness would be a good word. Strength would be another. With your two hands you were able to hold everything, bring it all together effortlessly. You never looked more beautiful."

He was quiet after that. Everyone waited for him to say something more, even while he sipped his drink, but after a while it became obvious that he was done. It took Tim to break the silence.

"How was that a bad thing?"

Mitch shook his head. "It was a fine thing. But it had nothing to do with me. That complete, perfect little scene was all her. It was her world. Even laying there I felt like I was viewing it from a distance. I was intruding, I didn't really fit."

"Why not?" Patricia again.

"Because I could never be in her life the right way."

"What was the right way?"

He knew why Liz loved these girls so much. They were all so sharp. She didn't have to ask a single question. She could just sit back and listen, knowing they would leave no stone unturned.

"All the way. To be in her life I had to walk all the way in, close the door behind me and lock it." He shifted in his seat. "I had to leave all my own problems, all my worries behind. I couldn't do that."

He didn't have to imagine how strange that must have sounded. It showed on the faces of the people around the table, although Patricia looked less puzzled than most of the others. When she asked, "Were you that attached to them?" the sound of her voice almost betrayed a certain understanding.

Mitch could only shrug after a while. "I don't know."

Madeline meanwhile, was more interested in the other part of his answer. "So, you thought you had to be all in," she said. "Okay, so why not? She's a good place to be."

Everyone laughed at that, even Mitch. But when they stopped laughing she was still waiting for his response. He only shook his head again and said, "I don't know. I was just absolutely certain that I would always be half in and half out."

He turned to Liz and pointed a finger in her direction. "You told me that yourself. More than once you said there was a part of me that always remained behind. You used to ask me why, remember? Well, I couldn't tell you then and I can't now, not even after all this time."

It was Patricia's turn at bat. "You were making it easy for yourself… in case you decided to leave. Or maybe you always knew you would."

He nodded. "But that's not a reason." After a moment he said, "There was no reason. That's just how it was." He turned to face Liz directly. "I knew I would make your complete life incomplete. I couldn't do that."

Finally Liz had a question of her own. "Even if I would

have accepted that? You never know. I might have."

"Yes," he said. "You would have. That was the whole problem. And once you had…" He let a wave of his hand complete the thought.

There were no more questions after that but no one seemed to know what to do next, so Mitch decided to cap it off with a grand gesture. He picked up his glass and held it up in Tim's direction.

"To Tim," he said, "Obviously a complete man."

Tim smiled and raised his glass in return. "To Mitch, obviously an honest man." He started to lower his glass, then raised it again. "For better or worse."

Everyone joined in the toast, touching their glasses and laughing. Then Liz turned back to Mitch and said, "Thank you, Mitch. Thank you for telling me that."

"You're welcome."

"Jerk."

He could only smile at that.

Exaggeration is a blood relation to falsehood
and nearly as blamable.
Hosea Ballou

Thirty minutes later Mitch was standing outside the gym. He felt a certain amount of loss as he stared at the blacktop under his feet and kicked at it with the toe of his shoe. Without trying he could recall a half-dozen memorable incidents that took place on that very spot twenty-five years before, when the whole area had been part of an enormous green field where he and his friends used to gather to play ultimate, hang out, stare at girls – anything but go to class.

But the field had been reduced to half its former size. What remained was just an island in the middle of a seemingly ever-growing parking lot.

But grass or no grass, he was feeling pretty good. Once his get-it-off-your-chest session was over he only had to excuse himself and walk a hundred feet, and just like that he had left Liz and her smart friends and all their smart questions behind. He assumed someone else at their table was taking their turn on the rack, and he wished whoever it was well.

But they were back there. They were inside. He was outside where a much simpler sort of reminiscing was going on, one which required far less soul-searching. If anything stood a chance of making him glad he came to this reunion, which he still doubted, it was this. At least it had more of a connection to his high school days.

That connection was the guys standing all around him in the field turned parking lot. Just as they had done twenty-five years before, their faces and the personalities behind them made him feel that he was tied into something worthwhile. For some reason, he didn't often think of them as his old friends, even though he referred to them that way in conversation. They were the people he had spent a lot of time hanging out with, cutting class with, getting high with, and so on. Perhaps that's what old friends were, but he was never really sure.

But one thing he could be sure of - none of them was likely to put him on the spot, at least not the way Liz had. But they weren't beyond putting him on a different kind of spot. Whereas Liz had boxed him in, left him with nowhere to go but straight ahead, his old Buddy Joe left him free to go wherever he chose by asking him a single question. "So, what have you been up to lately?"

Mitch had almost forgotten how well known he was for telling entertaining stories in high school. They all were really, but if it was a contest, Mitch was the clear winner. The subject didn't even matter - a trip he took to Washington, D.C. was as good as his mother flipping out because he accidentally knocked over a quart of milk. It could have been true, it could have been bullshit. They couldn't have cared less. They just loved the way he told a story, the way he put a spin on everything.

He had almost forgotten all about it because he never again found a ready-made audience to rival that one after high school. But apparently they hadn't forgotten. One after the other they reminded him of some of his best numbers. Remember the time you said you were dying... Oh, oh, remember the one about the dog with three legs... Man, the story about Principal Decker getting caught with Lisa Carroll in his office, remember that?

Yes, he did. The more of his old stories they brought up, the more of them he actually did remember. Before long he was laughing right along with them, as if he too had only been in the audience when they were first told.

What happened next was predictable. It took only a few minutes for someone to prompt him. Joe had asked the same question of a number of people that evening. "So, what have you been up to lately?" But when he asked Mitch, what he really meant was, "Tell us a story."

That time he didn't need to be pushed. He didn't need to struggle with the consequences of sharing a truth or changing anyone's life. In fact, his biggest struggle was simply coming up with something to say, and to his relief something that had happened to him came to mind right away. Only it wasn't much of a story, in his view. Although – and here is where he began to remember his tradecraft – by keeping the humorous facts, filling in the spaces with new, more interesting facts, and stretching the whole damned story until it was almost unrecognizable, it might just do.

This is how I used to tell a story, he thought as he began. It was just to get a laugh. It isn't like I'm giving testimony or something. It isn't like I'm lying to someone who only wants to hear the truth. I can exaggerate, or I can even make the whole damned thing up. What the hell does it matter?

"Man, the craziest thing happened on the way over here tonight. I was standing there waiting to use an ATM. It was... you know, one of those kiosks with one machine all by itself in a little eight-by-eight glass room, only one person goes in at a time while everyone else waits outside for their turn. You know the kind.

"So, that's what I was doing, waiting outside. Then the girl using the machine ahead of me finished her business, and I stepped back to hold the door for her. But then, just as she walked past me she rolled her eyes and said, "Better hold your breath."

"She said that to you?" asked Joe.

"Uh, huh, as she walked by."

"I don't even want to guess what that was all about." That came from Pierre - tall, interesting Pierre, who Mitch had always thought of as the smartest of his friends who didn't care at all about being smart.

"I didn't either, but I had to wonder... good luck with what? I hoped there wasn't a problem with the machine smoking or burning up or something after I'd been waiting to use it. But as soon as I stepped inside and let the door close behind me... oh man, then I know right away what she was talking about. It reeked in there. I mean, it was like that time we saw Cheap Trick in Hartford, remember? When everyone up in the nosebleed seats was...?"

That got a good response. "When everyone around us was getting high?"

"Yeah, it smelled just like that."

"It smelled like pot in the ATM vestibule?"

"Yeah, big time. Someone had definitely ducked in there to light up not long before. Anyway, there was nothing to do but move fast before I got the smell all over me. So that's what I did, I moved fast. I got what I needed, then I turned right around and headed for the door.

"Only by then there was someone waiting outside to come in and use the machine after me."

"Tell me it wasn't a cop," said Eddie, another of those really smart non-smart guys.

"Ha! No, it wasn't a cop." Mitch wondered why he hadn't thought of that.

"It was a lady. An older lady, maybe sixty-five. All I could think was, is she gonna think it was me? Like, is this woman actually gonna think I was lighting up in there? That would be kind of embarrassing."

"No shit. So what did you do?"

"What could I do? I had to get the hell out of there – I was done, and she had to get in. So I decided to have a little fun. I did the same thing the girl before me did, but with a little twist. When I opened the door I rolled my eyes and said, 'Better hold your breath.' And then I added, 'I didn't finish it all. I left it on the counter. There's matches, too.' And then I walked away. Fast."

"What did she do?"

"You got me, I never turned around to see her reaction."

"I wonder if she even went in. She probably got scared and went to a different ATM." Laughs.

"Man, I'll bet she went right in and looked for it." More laughs.

"I wouldn't be surprised if the girl ahead of you was the one lighting up and she was just playing innocent." Even more laughs.

That was it. That was the whole story and it did the trick. He was amazed at how fast and how easily he had come up with it. Apparently, it was like riding a bike. Maybe. Or maybe he wasn't as out of practice as he thought. It occurred to him that he had probably used those same skills countless times in countless situations over the years without even realizing it – getting out of work, breaking dates, over-selling himself on interviews, and so on. If so, he couldn't recall having to tell himself that it wasn't lying each and every time, but maybe he had.

He remembered feeling back in school that he was not the natural storyteller he was made out to be, that his reputation had come about accidently somehow. But he was the only one. Everyone else thought of it as a central part of his character. Whether they were right or not, his skills never seemed to fail him – not in school, and apparently not then, either.

For the time being at least, having come through he was no longer on the spot. The conversation moved on, and someone else took over holding court. There was only one more question that remained about his story and it was his own - how much of what he had just said was real? What part of it actually happened? He didn't even have to think about it.

He remembered walking into an ATM kiosk years before that smelled a little like pot, or parsley, or maybe carpet cleaner. But, that was it. There was no girl in there before him, no woman after. There were no conversations at all. All the rest was his imagination doing its thing.

As he thought back on most of his old stories that the guys had reminded him of, he had to admit there had been about that much truth to each of them on average - not really a concern for a storyteller, but for a guy just talking to his friends? So the question was, which was he when was busy not being smart in high school, a storyteller or a liar?

For that matter, what was he that night? Was he an entertaining old friend just pulling people's legs for the fun of it, or was he some guy who was so full of it he didn't know where the truth began or ended?

He made a mental note to give that some more thought, although he wasn't sure he would believe anything he had to say about it.

Speak the truth, but leave immediately after.
Slovenian Proverb

Mitch had always found that the most serious moments, the most dramatic moments, even the most enjoyable moments were the hardest to sustain. They never lasted as long or got as far as they might have, not because of anything the participants did or didn't do, but because the rest of the world always seemed to conspire to fuck them up. No one ever left you alone when you were having a truly great moment, except in movies.

In reality, someone always came over to tell you a stupid joke just as you were convincing a beautiful girl that you were worth talking to. Someone always kicked the back of your chair during the most intense scene in a movie. The phone always rang during sex.

But, that was life. At least, that was how he chose to look at it. In his view it was far more practical to expect to be interrupted at all the wrong moments than to try to live life in an isolation booth, and far less maddening. Besides, where would the spontaneity be in that?

But, for every rule there are exceptions, and Mitch believed he was experiencing one a bit later that evening. He found himself engaged in a deep moment that had somehow been carved out of an otherwise mostly shallow night, and he wanted nothing more than for it to play itself out uninterrupted. And for once it seemed that was exactly what was going to happen.

He was sitting with Bill Fiorentino in Bill's car at the far end of the parking lot. They had bumped into each other about fifteen minutes earlier, soon after Mitch went back into the gym and they got to talking. At one point, Bill asked if Mitch would mind walking while they talked. He wouldn't mind at all, Mitch assured him. In fact, he was only too glad to leave the gym. He was enjoying their conversation and was sure that if they stayed there surrounded by so many people they were bound to be interrupted at any moment.

They started off wandering aimlessly around the halls for a while until that somehow turned into wandering aimlessly around the grounds. They walked and talked through the basketball courts and the picnic area. They walked the length of the football field and across the courtyard. They walked until they found themselves with nothing left to walk aimlessly through but the parking lot.

They wound up there for no particular reason that Mitch could recall. But just then Bill suddenly declared, "Oh, there's my car." He unlocked the doors and said, "Let's sit in here for a while, what do you say?" Of course, the more casual he tried to make that sound the more sure Mitch was that Bill probably knew where he was headed all along, and that he probably had something specific he wanted to talk about once they got to the car. And he also guessed – correctly, as it turned out - that the car, a very flashy new Mercedes was like a visual aid or a key piece of scenery. Bill used it to set the tone.

Mitch didn't mind feeling that he had been handled a bit. After all, Bill had pretty well managed to cut them off from everyone and everything. No one was likely to walk up and interrupt their conversation there. If that's what it took to successfully engineer a rare unmolested moment to talk, so be it.

But having done so, what did Bill want to talk about? Well, as it turned out, he wanted to talk about Bill. Mitch had his own take on Bill that evening, a take he was not about to share out loud. Unnerved was not too strong a word to describe how he felt when he first laid eyes on him, although he would have been hard pressed to say why, exactly. The fact was, Bill looked pretty good. That wasn't something Mitch could have said about more than a handful of the other forty-somethings in the room. And whereas even those lucky few looked good but different, in Bill's case, he didn't even seem to have changed much, if at all.

He still had all the good looks he had ever had, which was considerable, and his natural aura of entitlement hadn't gone anywhere. He still seemed to fill the room with personality upon entering it. It was easy for Mitch to recall how when he and all their friends had struggled with being gangly, awkward seventeen-year-olds Bill already had a look that was impossible for them not to envy.

Back then, none of them would have dared take their shirts off on even the hottest day for fear of revealing their scrawny torsos except for Bill, who had a body that could have graced the cover of a surfer magazine. They all wore the same off-the-rack t-shirts and jeans, but his always fit as though they had been tailored. Even his smile looked custom-made for Hollywood while everyone else sported a mouthful of braces.

Naturally, quite a few of the guys tried to copy him. Not only did they get nowhere, but they also exhausted themselves in the process. The smarter ones like Mitch could see the irony in that. They understood that everything that went into being Bill came naturally to him. He just woke up each morning, and there it was - that was the whole point.

Looking at him all those years later, he could still believe that. And yet, when Bill first came over to shake his hand Mitch's first thought was not about what came naturally to him, but about what had been taken from him. Something seemed to be missing, something had been removed. It was as though he had taken three or four years for every one he was allowed, and now he was overdrawn, or used up. It doesn't show on the outside, at least not yet, but I can see it, he thought. He's rotting from the inside out.

Mitch knew he could be wrong. Judging his friend by what he saw in the harsh light of the parking lot lamps might not be fair. But when Bill said, "Man, you wanna hear something amazing?" Mitch gained a new respect for his own insights.

Bill's own take on Bill went further than Mitch's imagination ever could have. He was right, what he had to say was amazing.

He had gone off to Virginia after high school in order to study finance, and didn't return until he had his MBA. That much Mitch remembered. It seemed like the obvious choice for a guy with Bill's personality. Working on Wall Street was looked upon as stuffy, old man stuff when they were growing up, but by the mid-eighties all that had changed. Somehow, it had started to seem like the hip, sexy thing to do and Bill was drawn to it.

They saw each other only once after high school, sometime in the late nineties. Completely by chance, they met up in Grand Central Station while they were each waiting for a different train. They had only ten minutes together – just time enough to trade fast stories about their work and their families, lament that no one ever got in touch or kept tabs, then shake hands warmly and go their separate ways.

As incidents go, it was small, insignificant, even forgettable. And yet, that was where Bill chose to begin his tale.

"Do you remember that day in Grand Central? When I bumped into you?"

"Sure."

"I wish we had had more time then. There was stuff going on... lots of stuff. I remember when you split I wanted to ask if you could hang out and talk a while and take a later train."

Mitch found that surprising. "Really? Well, why didn't you?"

"I really wanted to talk then, get a few things out in the open. It would have been good... for me, I mean."

"Well, why didn't you say so?" Mitch asked again.

"Would you have stayed, or were you in a hurry?"

Mitch laughed. "How the hell would I know? That was years ago. I have no idea where I was even going."

Bill rolled his eyes. "Yeah, of course. What am I saying?"

But Mitch wanted to give a nicer answer than that. "But if I could have of course I would have stayed. Of course."

Bill liked that answer better. "Yeah? Thanks, I appreciate that. It would have been... good."

He reached out almost absentmindedly and turned on the radio. A classical music station came on and he turned it down low.

"This okay?" he asked.

"Sure, sure. Whatever you like. What was it you wanted to talk about, anyway? At Grand Central, I mean."

Bill looked thoughtful for a moment, then simply launched into a story. Mitch had no idea if any or all of it related to that meeting at Grand Central. But as Bill sat staring straight ahead, what Mitch could see of his expression told him that he should interrupt as little as possible.

"I've never liked any movies I've seen about Wall Street. Not a single one. I can't help nit-pick, you know? I feel like a soldier watching a movie about a battle he actually fought in, and being bothered because they got the terrain all wrong or dressed the extras in the wrong kinds of uniforms or something.

"There's always this attempt in those movies to show frenzy, or desperation... whatever it is they that think goes on there. And then the introspection - people staring at their reflections in coke mirrors, talking to themselves, pondering the depths they've sunk to or trying to remember the nice altar boys they were before greed got a hold of them. You know the kinds of shit I mean. But, it's all such crap. Know why?"

Mitch ventured a single word. "Why?"

"Because it's like a rattle snake, or a grizzly bear, or a fucking tractor trailer truck... if you could see it coming, you would move, wouldn't you? There's no deep thinking involved in destroying your own life. No philosophizing. That comes later, when it's too late to do you any good."

Mitch said nothing that time.

"Back then, when I saw you in the city, those were good times. I mean, if you call having everything you want to have and doing everything you want to do good times, well then... times were very, very good.

"I was married. I don't remember if I told you that then. My wife, Susan was a lawyer - had been, anyway. By then we had two little girls and Susan didn't work anymore. She was a terrific mother. And the girls, well...

"Like I said, you don't see it coming. Everything seems to come right out of the clear blue. So, one day right out of the clear blue Lisa, our youngest picked up something that fell out of my pocket and put it in her mouth. And then..."

He paused only for a moment, but then carried on in the same voice.

"Within oh, I'd say a week, the good times were over. I was moved out. Kicked out, really. Susan had gotten herself a divorce lawyer, and I had seen my girls for the last time without a court-ordered social worker present."

For the first time since he started talking, Bill turned to face Mitch.

"It was crack. The thing that fell out of my pocket. Just a small rock, but when Lisa put it in her mouth..." He shook his head. "She didn't swallow it, you see. Susan saw her and took it out right away. That's why... that's why she's still alive. That's why I'm not in jail right now for manslaughter or hanging from the end of a fucking rope."

He let out a sigh, then faced forward again.

"Susan knew how much coke I did. Before that, I mean. Everyone did it in those days, even her before the girls came along. She knew the lifestyle. That's what we called it. Frankly, that's how we looked at it – not drugs, not habits, but a lifestyle.

"Hookers were part of that, too. I mean, she knew we hired hookers to entertain clients all the time. You took rich old fuckers to strip clubs and got them laid, that's what you did. I mean, sure I had a taste now and again. Somewhere in the back of her mind I knew she knew that. She had to. Everyone did it. It was just..." He shrugged after a moment.

"The lifestyle," Mitch offered.

"Right. Normal stuff as far as we were concerned. Manageable stuff. Nothing to worry about. You understand? Until that... until that happened it was good times. I can still remember thinking as we were sitting with my daughter in the emergency room, we'll get through this. It's a bump in the road, nothing more. I just got a little sloppy, but these are good times so everything will be fine.

Then a week later I got to read a couple of paragraphs about myself in the complaint Susan filed with her lawyer. It came to me in the mail one day just like any other piece of junk mail. It said I had a two-thousand dollar a week crack habit. It said I had abused every drug under the sun at one time or another, including heroin. It said I had fallen way behind on most of my financial obligations, including my mortgage. It said I had a girlfriend named Natalia who lived in the Bronx in an apartment that I paid for, and who called my wife to harass her regularly. It said I was an absent husband and that my children hardly ever saw me and barely knew me and that I had been physically abusive to my wife on numerous occasions. There were police reports and emergency room pictures going back more than a year to back that up."

When he didn't continue right away Mitch asked, "Police reports? So then at least some of that was true."

"Some of it? It was all true."

"The drugs? Abusing your wife?"

"Yup. All of it."

"And yet you thought you were living in good times?"

"The best. Everything was just perfect. I was sure of it."

"So the divorce, all the rest of it, that took you by surprise?"

"Completely."

"How can that be?"

He shrugged again. "Some words you just have to live, my friend, before you can really claim to know what they mean. Love is one. Denial is another."

Part of Mitch wanted to ask how things stood then. What, if anything had worked out? Was he drug free? Did he ever speak to his daughters? But on the chance that the answers wouldn't be good, he didn't ask anything.

Bill pointed to the gym.

"I don't know how many people I spoke to in there tonight. Twenty. More, maybe. 'What have you been up to?' was the first question they all asked. You'd think that answering that question would be like running through a minefield or something, but it's not. It's actually pretty easy to just skate right by all of... that. Each time someone asked I answered the same way. I talked about everything that happened in my life up until that point because it's interesting enough. After that, all I had to do was say something obvious about the trials of raising teenage daughters and just like that a whole decade was accounted for. Then I asked how they were doing and I was off the hook. Home free."

"You didn't do that with me."

"No. I'm sorry."

"Don't be."

"The thing is, I lied to myself about this for years. And now, well now I lie to everyone else, instead. I guess you could call that progress. I'm not really sure. Only sometimes I feel that if I don't let it out, if I don't speak the words out loud I might just start believing my own bullshit again, you know what I mean?"

Mitch knew exactly what he meant. "Well, I'm glad you did. I'm glad I was here to listen."

"And, can all of this be between…"

"Between us? Of course. You don't even have to ask."

Bill nodded. "Thank you." Then he said, "So many of them in there are just dying to go home with a story, you know? They'll take any story that's worse than theirs. I read somewhere that people only go to their reunions in order to feel better about themselves. They want to see who got fatter than them, who lost more hair, who married a worse shrew."

They both laughed at that.

"I almost feel selfish keeping my story from them. Hearing it would make them all feel better about themselves, don't you think? 'At least I'm not like Bill,' they could say. 'We're blessed, aren't we, Dear because we didn't throw our lives away the way Bill did.'"

That went some way to explaining how haunted Bill looked, Mitch thought. No doubt it had to be tough for a one-time Golden Boy to see nothing but a train wreck when he looked in the mirror. But it must have been even tougher living with the fear that everyone else would see it, too. Like he said, the deep thinking and philosophizing came later. Bill was clearly living in later.

Mitch wished he could think of something to say to lighten Bill's load, any little thing that might make him feel safer, even for a little while. He suddenly remembered a few bits of gossip that had been circulating earlier about some of the unfortunates who couldn't attend, and he seized on it. "They've got other stories to take home," he said. "They won't miss yours, don't worry. Remember Thomas O'Donnell?"

"No."

"Big guy, originally a year ahead of us but he wasn't too sharp. He graduated with our class."

Bill shook his head. "I don't remember. Why, is he here?"

Mitch laughed. "Well, he bought a ticket alright, but he didn't make it. He became a gym teacher. I'm not sure where. Oklahoma, I think. Anyway, he got busted last month with one of his fifteen-year-old students."

"No shit?"

"Yup."

"Damn, that's bad."

"Oh, yeah. The funny thing is, no one would have even known about it, except that he tried to get his money back for the ticket and someone googled his name to look up his address. They came across an article about it, and that was that."

"Holy crap."

"And that's not all. One of the guys was telling me earlier about a friend of his - I don't even know his name. He couldn't come because his wife would find out she was actually his second wife."

Bill chuckled. "What? What do you mean?"

"Yeah, apparently he was married for a short while when he was in his twenties and he never bothered to tell this one about it. The only problem is that a bunch of people here knew him then, him and his first wife, so…"

"Oh, my God," Bill said. "Skeletons in the closet. Well, I sympathize with the poor bastard." A moment later, he added, "But man, that's funny as hell."

Mitch turned to see a broad smile on Bill's face. He didn't know what difference a single smile could make to someone carrying such an enormous burden, but he was glad to see it all the same.

And that seemed to him like a good note to end on. The moment had run its course and come to a decent end all on its own. He tapped his old friend on the knee.

"Come on. Let's go back in."

But as he opened the door and stepped out Bill started the car.

"No, I don't think so," he said. "I think I've contributed all I can to this affair."

He stretched out his hand to Mitch. "And I got far more than I expected. Thank you."

"You're welcome," Mitch said, shaking his hand.

Bill stared at him for a moment, smirking. "What a world," he finally said.

"What a world."

A moment later the Mercedes pulled away, and Bill was gone. Mitch lingered in the parking lot for a moment, wondering if he felt like going back in, either.

He was amazed that they had been able to spend that much time together and share that much without once being interrupted. That alone was more than he would have expected to get out of the evening, if he had even known to expect anything at all.

As for making a contribution, it certainly wouldn't have occurred to him before Bill said it that anyone was expected to contribute anything to such an evening, or that revealing a difficult truth counted. Thinking back over all the words he had spoken that night, he wondered about the value of his own contribution so far and what, if anything he still owed.

END

If You Don't Mind

MICHAEL CANAVAN

Matt was finding it hard not to be distracted. There were so many things to think about that his mind was positively begging to be set loose to wander. He had to keep reminding himself to stop - stop thinking about all that other shit and concentrate.

Yes, the building was in a beautiful location, and a daily drive there through the suburbs of Westchester would be almost too enjoyable to call a commute. Yes, the cafeteria with its restaurant-worthy menu and outdoor seating was a great perk. And yes, the office that would be his if he got the job had a full wall of floor-to-ceiling windows that looked out over an acre of tree tops.

Yes, all that was true. But it was also true that the woman sitting across from him wasn't finished yet. She began the meeting by promising that she would need to take up no more than twenty minutes of his time, and she still had a bit to go. And, if she had more questions to ask then he still had to come up with decent answers to each and every one of them if any of this was to have anything to do with him. So, he reminded himself again to cool it as he uncrossed one half-numb leg and crossed the other.

The woman sitting across from him - Andrea Kelly from Human Resources. All twenty-five or twenty-six years of her, he guessed. If he was right, that would make her about half his age. Of all the thoughts that had threatened to distract him, none had done nearly as good a job as that - I'm being interviewed by someone half my age. That realization had nearly derailed him completely, that and its companion thought - was she thinking the same thing? And if she was, what if anything did she make of the fact that she was interviewing someone twice her age?

But those were just thoughts, as I said. His thoughts. In spite of all his furious guessing, what Andrea may or may not have been thinking was completely unknown to him.

For all he knew, she didn't even know his exact age any more than he knew hers. She hadn't asked him, of course. She couldn't. But he could easily imagine her making a fairly good guess as they spoke - the dates that peppered his resume like a mine field would have made that easy. For that matter, all she really had to do was look at him. He had only the one face to trot out for her and while he may have looked pretty good for a man in his early fifties, he was still a man in his early fifties and that would have been clear to no one faster than a woman in her twenties.

But his exact age, and hers for that matter, was beside the point. It was enough that she was young and he was not. That was the first thing that came to mind when he was introduced to her at the door to her office, and for some reason that he couldn't fathom, it still lingered there. The difference in their ages mattered to him. From that first moment it mattered so much that he found himself making a conscious effort not to come off as old, or older, or whatever – not that he even knew what that meant or how he might possibly keep from doing it.

His first thought was simply to avoid using language that might make him sound dated, so he made a quick mental list of the phrases and words that usually brought him amused looks whenever he used them in front of his niece, Julia. He decided that under no circumstances would anything be groovy or dynamite for the duration of the interview. Nor would anything be bogus or slick. For that matter, he wouldn't be down with anything, he wouldn't dig anything, and nothing would be a drag.

For the most part he had no trouble sticking to these spontaneous rules. It wasn't as if he ever really used much of that crap anyway, except when Julia was around, and then mostly just to try and get a rise out of her. But there were violations. The first and most frequent was his use of the word dynamite. He found that he simply couldn't help himself - apparently it was a word he liked to use more than he realized. The building was dynamite. The office was dynamite. Even the work he would be doing was dynamite. Andrea said nothing to make him think there was a problem with that or any other word he used, but he still cursed himself each time he heard himself say it.

But more troublesome than any particular words were some of the anecdotes he told, which he was sure didn't help matters at all. That surprised him because he was normally pretty good at knowing what to say, knowing what would go over well in conversation. But for some reason in that room he only seemed to understand how something was going to sound after he had already said it. A number of times during the short meeting he caught himself making references that went right over Andrea's head because they predated her.

Even to his own ears he sounded like a history professor each time he had to stop and explain what the hell he was talking about – a humorless one, because of course nothing that is meant to be funny ever is funny once it has to be explained.

But by the time he was uncrossing and re-crossing his legs, when the interview was nearing the end he was feeling pretty good about the way things had gone overall, despite the unforeseen preoccupation with his age. He felt he had weathered that particular hiccup fairly well, in part because he had gone in riding pretty high on the success of his first two interviews of the day. Those interviews, with the people he would eventually be reporting to had gone even better than he could have hoped.

They were what mattered, he kept reminding himself. By contrast, the HR interview he was squirming through was more of a formality than anything else, twenty minutes devoted to double-checking facts and sizing up his personality. The real decisions would be made elsewhere - might already have been made, for all he knew.

No, he was doing well, he assured himself. If he was still feeling uncomfortable, it was not because so much was on the line just then, but because he was off his game. He had been caught off guard by his interviewer's youth, and by the fact that somehow, in some way, it meant something to him. But having recovered and dealt with it, he felt more himself. He was even feeling a bit philosophical about the whole thing by that point as he observed its impact on the way he felt, and on the nature of his conversation.

It was really only during the first part of the interview – there were three distinct parts, he later reflected – that the question of age took over his thoughts. Questions, really. Was there even an issue? If so, was there anything he could do about it? Was it something to hide, or something to flaunt? What did Andrea want to hear? And so on.

In the few seconds he had between meeting her at the door and sitting down to talk, he wasn't able to come up with answers to any of them, so he decided the only thing to do was to downplay the issue altogether – he wouldn't try to hide his age, but he wouldn't shout about it from the rooftops, either. So, in addition to watching his language, he attempted to keep his answers more or less date-neutral.

It was tiring work, he found. Since some stories only made sense in the context of when they occurred, he had to avoid them altogether. Others were okay once they had been tweaked a bit, but since he was editing himself on the fly, things could get pretty hairy pretty fast. He was doing so much omitting and transposing of dates that he soon had a lot to remember about what he had said just five minutes, or even five seconds before.

At times, it was hard for him to keep up with his own output and he slipped, like when Andrea mentioned that the company had recently gone through a building-wide update of their computers and he dragged out one of those should-have-thought-it-through-a-bit-more anecdotes.

"I swear," she said, "the computers we had before were so unreliable. Mine would crash so often that I never saved anything to my hard drive. I was too afraid I would lose it. I always worked right off the server, instead. It was like having no hard drive at all."

"Hm," Matt said with a smile. "Sounds familiar."

"Yeah? You had a computer that crashed a lot?"

"No, no… I had one with no hard drive."

She looked at him and tilted her head, waiting for more.

"I mean, that's the way it was supposed to be. It didn't come with one. It was a Macintosh, the first model. They had no internal hard drives."

"No hard drive?"

"Nope."

"Really? How did that work? Like, how did you store programs? How did you save anything?"

It could happen just that easily… he only had to utter a few careless words and he could find himself in exactly the position he didn't want to be in - explaining the past to her. And he certainly couldn't blame her for the questions she asked. He was the one that brought it up. All he could do at that point, aside from kick himself, was try to make his answers as short and uninteresting as possible so they could move on.

He shook his head. "It was completely low-tech. You stored everything on a floppy disk." With a laughed, he added, "You had to boot up from one, too. Not very advanced stuff."

"A floppy disk?"

"Uh, huh. You could only store a little over a single mega-byte on one of those things, if you can believe it."

"Why not use a CD?"

He scolded himself again. You had to go there, you idiot? But all he could do was continue. "They had no CD drives," he admitted as cheerfully as he could manage, "Just that... the floppy."

After a moment she said, "Wow, I've never heard of anything like that."

He could have left it there, could have just admitted to losing that round, but instead her words gave him an idea, and that idea became something of a way out. "Neither had I when I first came across it," he said. "They had one in the mail room of a company I used to work for. They used it for simple stuff - printing out shipping labels, that kind of thing. I can remember asking the same question as you, 'How does this thing work?' I never really understood it, but it did the job. They used it all the time."

He was happy with that bit and he awarded himself a mild pat on the back for having come up with it. It put some distance between him and the dinosaur computer, as if he knew barely more about it than she did, and even shared completely in her awe of the prehistoric relic. It was untrue of course, but the fact that the only Macintosh he had ever used was one he had owned himself and used all through college was information for another time and place.

He allowed himself an even more enthusiastic pat for not digging the hole any deeper than he did, which he very easily could have done. There were a dozen different stories he might have told regarding computers before he decided on the one about the Macintosh, each one worse than the one before. He doubted he would have been able to rescue himself quite that easily from a few of them.

Only once after that did he have any trouble with anecdotes, but it was that last one that led to the second part of the interview. The change-over was abrupt, and it came after Andrea made a casual remark about her father that was clearly intended to put the poor guy on one side of some invisible line, and Matt and herself on the other. It was because of the remark that the age issue finally evaporated. Once he found himself on the same side of something, anything as her, he no longer felt the same pressure to constantly try and bridge the gap he saw separating them.

While describing some of the more friendly, social aspects of the company to him, such as their softball team and their early-morning yoga classes, Andrea mentioned their most recent office Christmas party. She raved about the venue they had chosen, the food they had, and especially the DJ they had hired. She ran through a list of songs he had played for them to dance to while Matt nodded approvingly, and when she got to Every Little Thing She Does Is Magic, Matt said, "Oh, I like that song."

"Me too," she responded enthusiastically. "I think the Police made great records."

"They did, and they were a great live band, too. One of the

best I've seen."

"Oh? You saw them play? Where?" she asked brightly.

Again, it happened just that quickly. A few casual words, and there he was, back in the past. He was painfully aware that he was about to describe something that happened before she was born, but what could he do? There was no way to edit that one. "Shea Stadium," he said. "It was on their last tour, right before they broke up."

"Really? Oh, I'm jealous. I heard those Synchronicity shows were great."

He felt more than a little relieved by her response – since she was obviously aware that he was recalling ancient events there was no need for him to try and fudge any details. Plus, she clearly knew what he was talking about for once. So, rather than look for a way out he went the other way completely, and simply dove in head-first.

"They were. Those guys were thanklessly good."

"I'll bet."

"Yeah, it was something. I was on the second level but right up front by the railing so I could see over, you know? And the whole place was shaking from all the people dancing - you could actually feel it going up and down. At one point I was standing there looking down at the people below, and I was convinced the whole thing was just going to collapse at any minute, and we were all going to fall onto those poor guys below – the concrete, the seats, everything." He smiled. "Didn't happen, of course."

"That sounds pretty scary."

"Yeah, but then I suddenly remembered there were a lot more people above us. When I looked up, sure enough they were all shaking, too. Then I started thinking they might just come down on us. Now, THAT was scary."

She laughed at that. "Yikes! Well, I've got my own Police

story."

"Yeah?"

"Mm, hm. I saw them too, on their LAST last tour – the reunion tour."

"Really?

"Yup. As a matter of fact, I saw the very last show they played. The one at the Garden. It was just like you said, thanklessly good."

"Now, I'm jealous. I would have loved to see that."

"You would have loved it, alright. They played so many great songs, not just their big radio hits. And they actually did a couple of songs by Cream and Hendrix, too. You know, a famous trio covering other famous trios..."

Happily, the words, "Oh you know those bands?" didn't leave his mouth. Instead he said, "Oh yeah, I remember reading about that," which was true, and much smarter.

"Yeah, and they did a funny thing, too. When they went off stage before the encore Sting sat down and had his beard shaved off by these two women barbers while someone else gave him a manicure. It was hilarious. They actually showed the whole thing as it happened up on the big screens."

"You know something? At Shea they did something sort of like that - it wasn't even at the encore, it was right in the middle of the show. They just took a break and went backstage and had tea. Like, they actually sat down and had a whole tea service."

"Really?"

"Yeah, then they just came back out and went on with the show. It was really funny."

That was not the first time during the interview they had shared a few pleasant words, nor was it the first time they had drifted so far off topic. But it was the first time Matt felt that he could let his guard down without feeling threatened by whatever he might say next. Even though they were talking about two different events that took place at two different points in time, it was where the stories overlapped that mattered - what they had in common, not what separated them.

That short exchange went a long way towards putting him at ease. For the first time since he sat down he didn't feel quite as guilty about having been born when he was. But what she said next did much more - it made him feel that he'd been positively let off the hook.

"My father isn't into the Police," she said with a conspiratorial smile. "He always says he never understood where they were coming from. Can you imagine?"

"Where they were coming from? You mean the reggae thing?"

"Maybe that, maybe the blond hair or the punk thing... who knows? He actually had a chance to see them in eighty-three, the same tour you saw. My Grandmother told me all about it. She was going to treat him for his twentieth birthday, but he wasn't interested. She said she was surprised because she thought everyone liked the Police. But, not him. So she offered to get him a ticket to any show he wanted to see. You won't believe who he picked."

"Who?"

She tried to hold back, but then laughed. "I can't even say. It's too embarrassing."

"What? Come on. Who?"

"Prince."

"Prince!?"

"That's what my Grandmother said. 'Prince!?' But she bought him the ticket. My dad chose Prince at Radio City over the Police at Shea."

They laughed a bit more until Matt said, "Well, it's

probably not as bad as all that. I mean, Prince is great. I'll bet he put on a hell of a show."

Andrea looked skeptical.

"Okay, how about this," he offered, "your dad probably just wanted to check out Vanity in her lingerie."

She laughed again. "Yeah, probably. But there's no way around it, his taste in music is strange. And it's not just the Police - he isn't into any of the bands we would like."

That was it. With one quick sentence Matt was done thinking of everything that was said in terms of the years and what they meant, and the second part of the interview was ushered in. What signaled the change was subtle enough that Matt could have been forgiven for not even hearing it, but he did – all single solitary word of it. "We," she said, "...the bands we would like."

And because she uttered that word, the 'us and them' dynamic he had created and saddled himself with shifted in his favor, big time. What did it matter that he had only been elevated to 'us' level as a result of her father being demoted to the ranks of 'them'? It was still sweet.

His new-found status was confirmed, even given a serious boost a few moments later when she mentioned having seen another of her favorite bands at the Garden a few years before. With something approaching giddiness, he amazed her by revealing that he had been there on the very same night. They had the Rolling Stones in common, too. Not surprisingly, her father hadn't caught that one, either.

But the fact that Matt no longer felt he had to obsess over the years didn't stop him from being aware of them. For instance, according to Andrea's story, her father was celebrating his twentieth birthday in nineteen-eighty-three. That meant that in addition to assuming that he was twice her age, he now knew for a fact that he was older than her father.

Irrelevant as that bit of trivia may have been to an HR employee and a job applicant when you get right down to it, had he heard it just a few minutes earlier it probably would have hit him hard as evidence of... something negative. But by then he was able to view it quite differently. He may have been older than Andrea's father he told himself, but he was clearly cooler. That wasn't much of a boast in the grand scheme of things, he knew, but it would do. It was enough to sustain him for the few minutes that remained of the meeting, anyway.

And sure enough the next few minutes were easy for him. They were back on script and back to business as Andrea said what she had to say and asked what she had to ask, and Matt supplied appropriate answers in return. And that could have been that, and would have been except for another random sentence which brought about the third part of the interview.

It came as a surprise to him that there even was to be a third part, considering how well things were going. But in a way, one grew right out of the other – the fact is, he never would have done what he did next if he hadn't first gotten over his age obsession. He would have remained far too guarded.

But that only partially explained it. What really prompted him was not indiscretion, but a sense of pride. What he said was not the result of a slip, it was not one of his badly chosen anecdotes that he later wished he could take back. It was a choice. He went in with eyes wide open.

Matt was rather proud of his past, he was happy to discover. When Andrea stumbled onto a subject that touched on one of his proudest memories, he found that he wanted to join in, wanted to talk about it. More than that, he found that he didn't feel like cheating himself by altering it in any way. He had done enough of that over the course of their conversation, and he was feeling more than a little two-faced. The details of this story, whatever they said about him or his age, would just have to stand.

Again, it was just a few casual words from Andrea that caused things to shift. While they were talking about the cost of living in and around New York she mentioned that she had shared an apartment with two female roommates – something she didn't recommend - in Jersey City while a student at NYU because she couldn't afford to live in Manhattan.

She described their apartment as a fifth-floor walk-up which was originally a one-bedroom, but had been divided into three with the addition of a few walls which were as thin as paper. With a far-off smile, she added that even though she was always behind, always strapped, she still looked back on those years as some of the best of her life.

That was it, that was all she said. What came next would have been more understandable if she had been making some sort of comparison, or even if she had asked him his opinion, but she hadn't done either of those things. Her remarks had absolutely nothing to do with his own first apartment, any of his experiences, or even him, for that matter.

But for whatever reason, her musings on the subject got him started, and with his own far-off smile firmly in place he simply began talking even as he was asking himself why he was doing it. And for the first time since he walked through the door he spoke with absolutely no regard for how he sounded, or even how his words might date him.

"Roommates weren't an option when I got my first apartment. Everyone I knew was still seventeen like me, and still in high school."

"In high school?"

He nodded. "All except for me. I left." He paused, but just for a moment. "After a year or so I went back. I got my diploma from an adult high school so I could go to college. But at that point, at seventeen I felt I had to move out for... uh, various reasons, and that meant I had to work, so..."

She didn't say anything to that. Didn't raise an eyebrow. She just waited.

"But my apartment! It was a nice place, my first place, all things considered," he continued. "Not a walk-up, but a walk-down. A basement studio in the Bronx. And it had all the amenities, let me tell you - a hot plate, a toaster oven, and a sort of futon without a frame that could be folded into either a bed or a chair. All that, plus two little windows up towards the ceiling for two-hundred-and-twenty-five dollars a month - about half my take-home pay."

He was still smiling and so was she when she responded, picking up right where he had left off. "And, you had no roommates to deal with, coming and going all the time? And a bathroom all to yourself? It sounds charming." she said.

"It was. Oh, and I had a tv. A thirteen inch black and white job that got three or four channels on a good day, if I could manage to get the antenna lined up just right. The Bronx had no cable in those days – none of the other boroughs did, only Manhattan. Not that I could have afforded it anyway."

Did she understand what he meant by that? Did someone her age understand that cable service was not only a relatively new thing, but that it didn't just appear everywhere at once, like a new web site? That the cable actually had to be laid somewhere first, somewhere else second, and so on? He didn't know and he didn't care. He wasn't going to be doing any more explaining, not about the logic of offering cable service in densely populated areas first, or about anything else for that matter.

But whether she understood it or not, her next question had nothing to with that or anything else he had said. Instead, she went right beyond all that, and took him further into his story than he had intended to go.

"So you moved out quite young. Were on your own when you were in college?"

"You mean still living without roommates?"

"No, I'm sorry, I meant to say financially. Did you put yourself through college?"

"Oh, yes. Yes, I did."

She nodded. "That's admirable. It must have been tough."

Matt smiled again at that. He knew he could have said something as simple as, "Yes, it was tough going at first, but things eventually got better and all the hard work paid off in the end. You know, the American Dream and all that…" If he left it there, his little story would have demonstrated some good qualities, like his independence at a young age and his ability to overcome obstacles. It would have even made him look a bit sympathetic to his interviewer, which never hurts.

But he was still smiling. He could feel his smile, and he knew what it meant. She had started him looking inward, and now he felt like turning himself inside-out, at least for a few more moments. So without giving it another thought he simply started telling her something he thought about from time to time, but hadn't told anyone else in decades.

"Yes, it could be. What made it tough mostly was just how young I was, you know? I wasn't naïve, but I was… well, at seventeen I had very little experience. I was doing everything for the first time, learning all these important lessons more or less on the fly. It was like…"

"Baptism by fire…" she offered.

"Precisely." He leaned forward in his chair. "I remember

185

the day I learned a little something about budgeting, for instance. This was a Monday afternoon, maybe a month after I had first moved out. I was about to get the train home from lower Manhattan where I worked but I needed to buy a token, so I stopped first to count the money I had in my pocket - four dollars and fifty cents. That meant I had four dollars and fifty cents to my name. Period. No savings, nothing hidden in my sock drawer at home. Nothing but that.

"I started to do the math in my head. I wasn't going to get paid until that Thursday, so that money had to get me back and forth to work, feed me, and so on until Thursday afternoon. Well, the figuring didn't take very long."

"How much was the train then?" she asked.

"Seventy-five cents."

"And you needed to buy, what... six tokens to get back and forth to work until Thursday?"

"Exactly."

She quickly did the math, then laughed. "Oh my God, exactly four-fifty."

"Yup."

"So, what did you do?"

"What could I do? I bought six tokens. And then..." He almost winced at the memory, which didn't feel anything like thirty years old. "Then, I didn't eat for three days."

"You didn't... nothing at all?"

He shook his head. "Nothing. I had nothing at home, couldn't buy anything. The funny thing is there was almost always food around at work. I worked as a messenger then for a large law firm, and it seemed like every other day there would be extra bagels left over from breakfast meetings, or cake left over from birthday parties, that sort of thing. There always seemed to be food around, but that week... well, for whatever reason there was nothing at all that week."

"Oh, that's awful."

"Yeah, I was sort of counting on that."

He could still feel himself smiling, but maybe not quite as much, and he knew he was talking softer, more slowly. He still didn't care, so he went a little further.

"There was a room where all the messengers gathered when we weren't, you know, out delivering something, and there was a little radio in there that was always playing. Well, every time I finished one of my shifts I would hurry back there and get a seat as close as I could to that radio so that no one would hear my stomach grumbling. It worked pretty well."

"You must have been one very happy guy on Thursday," she said in a soft voice.

"By midday I was, yeah. Remember, there was no direct deposit then. There were no ATMs, no debit cards. I had to wait until eleven o'clock to actually get my paycheck, then wait another hour for lunch so I could go and stand on line at the bank to cash it.

"I can still remember there was this bowl of... oh, what were they called... Thin Mints! There was a bowl of Thin Mints on a counter in the bank. I must have eaten two dozen of those damned things while I stood on line."

She was quiet for a moment, then once again instead of going back to fill in any details he might have glossed over, she asked a question that moved the story ahead.

"I'm thinking about that first meal. What did you have?"

"For lunch?"

She nodded. "After the Thin Mints."

He held his hands about twelve inches apart. "A meatball hero... like this. I bought it right after leaving the bank. It was glorious, but I could barely get through half of it."

He paused for a moment, until he was sure he had reached

the end of his story. When he looked up at her his next words came automatically. "I'm sorry. That wasn't too relevant."

She was still smiling, but very softly. She shook her head and let out a quick laugh. "Neither were Prince or my Grandmother." Then she added, "That's an incredible story. But, it's very sad."

"Yeah? Well, it's okay, believe me. I've had a lot of meatball heroes since then. A lot of Thin Mints, too. Plus, like I said, I learned a lot. I even know how to budget now." That was a good line to end on. It got a relieved smile from both of them.

That was when he changed legs. That was when he started looking back over the meeting-in-progress and feeling pretty good about how it had all gone up to that point. That was when all the other distractions began begging for attention again, and when he did his best to ignore them and settle in for the last bits.

But as it happened, by that point their business was all but done. Andrea actually had very little, if anything left to ask. So, barely ninety seconds later he was standing by her office door again, shaking her hand for the second time. It seemed to him that a lot more than twenty minutes had passed since he had last stood in that spot. The whole interview-in-three-parts theory hadn't really gelled for him yet – not in any kind of detail, anyway - but he certainly felt like he'd been on one hell of a roller coaster ride.

As he made his way to his car he made a mental note to take some time later in the day to try and understand exactly what had come over him and why. But just then he was not in the mood to analyze himself. He was more interested in letting the distractions take over, finally.

He drove away admiring the building, the trees, even the

wall of windows that were part of the office which might just become his, looking down on all of it.

END

MICHAEL CANAVAN

ABOUT THE AUTHOR

Michael Canavan is a New York-born writer, graphic designer, and musician living in Connecticut. He has two children and one grandchild.

Made in the USA
Charleston, SC
25 April 2014